# What Was Annie Going To Do?

Dane was aggravating, exciting, compelling. She couldn't resist him. In her heart, she knew she'd said a fond goodbye to her memories of her late husband the first time Dane kissed her... because she was falling in love.

She should be happy. She should be ecstatic! He wanted to marry her. He desired her.

*But he didn't love her,* didn't even believe in love. He'd been clear about that. And worse yet, he didn't want her love. On the other hand, he was offering her a second chance at children of her own. She had no doubt he'd be a devoted family man.

But could she live without love?

Dear Reader,

This month's lineup is so exciting, I don't know where to start...so I guess I'll just "take it from the top" with our October *MAN OF THE MONTH*. *Temptation Texas Style!* by Annette Broadrick is a long-awaited addition to her SONS OF TEXAS series. I know you won't want to miss this continuation of the saga of the Calloway family.

Next, many of you eagerly anticipated the next installment of Joan Hohl's BIG BAD WOLFE series— and you don't have to wait any longer. *Wolfe Wanting* is here!

Don't worry if you're starting these series midstream; each book stands alone as a sensuous, compelling romance. So take the plunge.

But there's much more. Four fabulous books you won't want to miss. Kelly Jamison's *The Daddy Factor;* Raye Morgan's *Babies on the Doorstep;* Anne Marie Winston's *Find Her, Keep Her;* and Susan Crosby's *The Mating Game*.

Don't you dare pick and choose! Read them all. If you don't, you'll be missing something wonderful.

All the best,

Lucia Macro
Senior Editor

---

Please address questions and book requests to:
Silhouette Reader Service
U.S.: 3010 Walden Ave., P.O. Box 1325, Buffalo, NY 14269
Canadian: P.O. Box 609, Fort Erie, Ont. L2A 5X3

# ANNE MARIE WINSTON

## FIND HER, KEEP HER

SILHOUETTE *Desire*®
Published by Silhouette Books
America's Publisher of Contemporary Romance

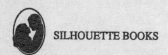

SILHOUETTE BOOKS

ISBN 0-373-05887-X

FIND HER, KEEP HER

**Books by Anne Marie Winston**

Silhouette Desire

*Best Kept Secrets* #742
*Island Baby* #770
*Chance at a Lifetime* #809
*Unlikely Eden* #827
*Carolina on My Mind* #845
*Substitute Wife* #863
*Find Her, Keep Her* #887

---

## ANNE MARIE WINSTON

A native Pennsylvanian and former educator, Anne Marie is a book lover, an animal lover and always a teacher at heart. She and her husband have two daughters and a menagerie of four-footed family members. When she's not parenting, writing or reading, she devotes her time to a variety of educational efforts in her community. Readers can write to Anne Marie at P.O. Box 302, Zullinger, PA 17272.

For The Boop—
the finest Maw-in-law a gal could ever have

# One

He would wring her beautiful neck when he caught her. Dane Hamilton sprinted down the tree-shaded block, cursing the August heat wave in Chicago and everything else in sight.

"Get back here, Miss—!"

But she just tossed a laughing glance over one shoulder and kept right on running.

Okay, fine. "I'm going home," he yelled after her. "I'm not chasing you one step farther. Do you hear me? *Not one step!* I don't care if you never come home!" Dane turned around and took several rapid strides back the way he'd come. He peeked over his shoulder.

She had stopped and was watching him. Little witch.

Dane kept on going. This was it. Absolutely it. He'd moved to River Forest, Illinois, only two weeks ago and he would bet all the neighbors thought he was crazy.

Come to think of it, he was. And undignified, to boot. Here he was, the new vice president of a local bank, chasing down the street after her. For the third day in a row.

He should have followed his instincts and gotten rid of her before he left Peoria. The trouble was, she was so damned cute. She'd wormed her way into his heart despite his reservations. If anything happened to her, he'd never forgive himself. His steps slowed. Maybe he should go back and try to catch her one more time. Maybe—

A cold, wet nose thrust into his palm. "Miss Mess," Dane said with fond exasperation. He hunkered down to nuzzle his face into the neck of the black Doberman that was gazing up at him with innocent eyes. While he hugged her, his hand caressed her neck, easing down to get a death grip on her collar before she realized it. "You're going to drive me insane," he told the dog.

With his hand firmly on her collar, Dane headed for home. Missy, her youthful energies apparently expended in the wild chase, trotted docilely beside him, the stump of her tail wagging madly. By the time they'd traveled three blocks, Dane was furious again. He was too tall to be comfortable in this position. His back was killing him.

As he rounded the corner and turned onto his own street, he saw the couple who lived in the corner house taking in groceries. Damn. The fellow had smiled tolerantly at him just yesterday when Dane was towing Missy home. The man's grin had been amused. And the woman...

*She was exactly what he was looking for in a wife.*

He assessed the petite lines of her figure just before she disappeared into the house, mildly surprised at the instant physical response the unknown woman aroused in him. He hadn't wanted a woman in a long time, even though he knew it was past time he got back to the business of finding a wife. But now...

He wanted. Oh, yes indeed, he wanted. And nothing would please him more than coming home every night to a woman who looked like this one. She was perfect.

At least, physically she was, with the kind of full hourglass curves that men loved and women constantly tried to diet away. She had a delicate little nose and sharply defined cheekbones. Her forehead was broad, her face heart-shaped.

He hadn't met her, so he didn't know if she possessed any of the qualities he'd come to realize were vital in a wife. But he could imagine himself coming home to this woman every night, tucking the children they'd have together into their beds before taking her to the larger bed in the room they'd share....

Too bad she was taken.

Nearly every day, he was conscious of his best years slipping away silently, uneventfully. He'd envisioned himself a father by the time he hit thirty-five, in love and happily married and raising the family of which he'd dreamed.

Well, it wasn't too late. He wouldn't let it be. Maybe the love part had turned out to be a royal joke, but he was determined to make the rest come true... on his terms. When he reentered the marriage sweepstakes, he would have his eyes wide open. He would marry for companionship and sexual compatibility.

And he would demand a sworn affidavit from his bride-to-be that she fully intended to present him with children as soon as possible after the wedding date.

Once again, the bitter taste of rage rose to taunt him. Maybe he wasn't ready to jump into another relationship yet.

Still, he thought, his eyes appreciatively scanning every curve as the woman made another trip from the house to the car, a man could enjoy. As she straightened up, the long, dark braid that started at the crown of her head slipped across her fanny, gently swishing back and forth with every step she took. As she disappeared into a side door with the man behind her, Dane let out his breath in a silent whistle. Yes, indeed, a man could enjoy.

Just as he drew even with their driveway, the man bounced through the screen door, letting it slam behind him. His red hair was a flaming halo backlit in the early-evening sun.

"Hello," he said. "Got a runaway, have you?"

Dane nodded.

"Patrick Murphy." The redhead was striding down the driveway, extending a hand.

Dane halted. He couldn't help but notice the slogan scrawled above the silhouette of a skier on the front of Patrick Murphy's T-shirt: Skiers Do It With

Poles. Nice, he thought with reluctant amusement, real nice. He was still bent over at an awkward angle, holding on to Missy's collar, but he extended his own hand. "Dane Hamilton."

When Patrick Murphy shook his hand, Dane winced. What kind of work did the guy do to have a grip like that? Unobtrusively, Dane flexed his mangled fingers.

"You moved in a few doors down, right?" Patrick said.

Dane nodded. "Yes, two weeks ago. I was fortunate to find a house in this neighborhood."

"Have you lived in the Chicago area long?" The redhead fairly radiated exuberant friendliness.

"No. I just moved from Peoria. I'm looking forward to getting to know my way around."

Patrick nodded. "I grew up in Chicago. It's a great town." He looked down at Missy. "Your dog?"

"Yeah. Miss Mess, meet Mr. Murphy."

"Mind if I pet her?"

When Dane indicated his assent, Patrick extended his fisted hand for Missy to sniff. She evidently took it as a sign of encouragement. Before Dane could stop her, she leaped at Patrick, her huge front paws planted firmly on his chest. Patrick didn't appear to mind, crooning ridiculous baby talk to her as she licked his face with great, sloppy swipes of her tongue. It occurred to Dane that he must sound exactly the same sometimes.

The screen door slammed again. Over Patrick's shoulder, Dane saw the woman he'd been watching.

She hesitated when she saw Patrick with him, then slowly she walked down the driveway.

"Hello," she said.

Up close, Dane could see that her eyes were big and blue, serious eyes that didn't match the half-hearted smile she was aiming his way. This close, he could see that her hair was a dark, coppery red. She wore it all pulled back in the braid except for some wispy bangs. Her mouth was wide and she had a hint of an over-bite that only added to his overall impression of cute and cuddly. He wondered if she was Patrick's wife.

If she was, he got a ten in the Great Taste Ratings.

He cleared his throat, aware that he'd been staring. "Hello."

Patrick waved an arm at him, craning his neck away from the dog's incessant licking. "Annie, this is Dane Hamilton. He's our new neighbor." Missy licked Patrick right across the lips and he sputtered. "All right. That's enough kissing for me."

Annie. It suited her.

"Still a puppy, isn't she?" Annie said, eyeing Missy critically.

Dane nodded ruefully. "I'm afraid so. About ten months old."

"She's a real beauty. Is she registered?"

"Yes. She came from a line of champions bred at a kennel in Bolingbrook. She was a birthday present from my parents." Dane shook his head. "I doubt I'd have kept her if I'd known I would be moving to Chicago. My home in Peoria had a huge, fenced yard. I'm having a terrible time keeping tabs on her here. I've been trying to train her to come when I call, but so far I haven't had much success.''

Patrick groaned. "Now you've done it."

Dane looked at him quizzically, then at Annie.

Patrick looked at her, too, and Dane envied them the unspoken communication in the wordless exchange. Then Patrick said, "Do you want to tell him or shall I?"

Annie gave a small shrug of her shoulders and turned back to Dane. "I'm a dog trainer. She's the perfect age for a Basic obedience course, if you're interested."

She was a *dog trainer?* Somehow, Dane couldn't envision this tiny, delicate woman handling big, bouncy dogs likes Missy. But still...dog obedience school might not be a bad idea. "Would she come when I called her then?"

"Eventually. How obedient your animal becomes is due, in large part, to how consistent you are with your training." Her eyes slid to Patrick. "My brother, for instance, can't bring himself to slip a training collar on a dog, let alone actually use it."

Patrick shrugged. "I'm softhearted. What can I say?"

Annie narrowed her eyes at him. "You could say that you know that dogs have very strong, muscular necks and the collars don't harm them."

"Wait a minute." Dane stared at them. "You two are brother and sister?" As he studied them, he could see a resemblance. Something about the eyes...

Annie nodded, distracted from what was apparently a familiar argument.

"Everyone says I'm better-looking." Patrick patted his own chin fondly.

His sister shook her head. "We allow him these little delusions," she said to Dane. Then her teasing manner faded and the serious expression returned. "Let me get you one of my business cards, in case you're interested in enrolling your dog in obedience classes." She turned to go back up the driveway.

Absently watching the twitch of her braid as she walked away, Dane said, "I thought you two were husband and wife." As she crawled into the passenger side, he could see the gently rounded curves beneath her white shorts, and he held his breath as the shorts inched higher, revealing smooth, tanned thighs.

Patrick cleared his throat loudly.

Dane jerked his gaze away from the view in time to note the amused sympathy in Patrick's green eyes. "Is your sister ... involved ... with anyone?"

"No." Patrick's eyes lost their humor. The single syllable sounded oddly flat. "Annie doesn't date."

*Doesn't date?* Dane considered the possible meaning behind the words. "Should I take that as a warning?"

Patrick shook his head and the friendliness returned, though a shadow still lingered in his eyes. "No. Just a fact. She's a widow."

*She's a widow.* Dane took the white card from his pocket and fingered the elegant gray lettering of the business card, which read: Evans' Canine Training School, A.E. Evans, Certified Instructor. All Levels of Puppy and Dog Obedience Classes Available.

It had been on the wide ledge above his kitchen window for three weeks. On the Wednesday evening after he'd met Patrick Murphy and his beautiful sister, he'd gone to a local department store and purchased a six-foot leash for Missy. Annie had suggested it, and he'd felt foolish after she'd explained that the only way to teach Missy not to run from him was to start from the beginning, to keep her on a leash all the time unless he tied her in the yard.

He'd called the number on the card and had gotten a recording asking him to leave his name and number if he was interested in the class schedule. As soon as he'd received the brochure in the mail, he'd enrolled Missy and himself in a beginners class that started the first week in September.

He hadn't even known Annie's last name until he'd seen it on her business card.

As he parked the car, he was conscious of a keen anticipation tightening his stomach muscles. He could attribute it to his desire to have his dog better trained, but he would be lying to himself.

He wanted to see Annie again. Tonight, at her fall orientation and open house, he would have the opportunity.

Every evening when he'd walked Missy, he'd watched for Annie when he came past her property, but he hadn't seen her since. He might not be looking for another wife yet, but he wasn't averse to some harmless flirtation, maybe a little dating that might lead to...well, what was the point in that kind of speculating? He would only drive himself crazy.

Maybe he'd imagined the sexual pull that had hit him deep in the gut the first time he'd seen her. Maybe she wasn't as great-looking as he remembered. Maybe—

Oh, hell. He hadn't imagined or exaggerated anything. Annie was waiting outside the door of her dog center, her hair braided in the same style it had been the first time he'd met her. She was tinier than he remembered, but every bit as appealing, with her lush curves and that indefinable something that told every male instinct he had to stand up and howl.

Too bad he didn't affect her the same way. Her blue, blue eyes were serious as she watched him approach, wary even. She didn't return his smile.

"Hi." Surely he could get her to relax her mouth from that straight, firm line. "You don't know how I'm looking forward to this."

"Don't expect miracles. Training a dog doesn't happen overnight, and it takes a lot of diligent work." She pointed to the fenced yard to the left of the training facility. "The grassy area is for the dogs to relieve themselves before and after class." As he moved toward the door, she added, "And over there's the shovel and the trash can for cleaning up."

So much for getting her to relax.

Once inside the building, he found a seat along the wall and waited. There was a large crowd, maybe seventy people, in the room. After a few more had come in, Annie entered and stepped to the middle of the floor.

"Good evening. Welcome to the Evans' Canine Training School. This is the orientation session for all seven of the upcoming Basic classes. I'm Annie Evans, and I'm a canine trainer certified by the National Association of Dog Obedience Instructors. For the next eight weeks, you and I will be working together to teach your dog basic obedience commands.''

So that was why there were so many people here. He was relieved that there wouldn't be seventy-plus dogs all in one class. He listened carefully as she explained the history of the canine, offered an overview of the training program and gave the group information on preventing dogfights for the first few weeks while the dogs were still unsocialized.

She was impressive in her professional mode. He didn't know what he'd expected but he suddenly realized he'd been thinking of her as a small, helpless creature who needed protection. Seeing her in this setting where she shouldn't fit so comfortably but did, he acknowledged to himself just how badly he wanted to get to know her.

''Now,'' she said, ''I know many of you think, 'My dog's never going to listen.' I'm here to tell you any dog can be trained. What it takes from you as a trainer is patience, persistence, consistency, and perhaps most important, love. I'm going to introduce you to several dogs and handlers who take classes here. Each will briefly demonstrate aspects of our obedience programs. As you watch these dogs, remember that they all started out with the same lack of skills that your dog has today. Obedience training and love are the combination that created the handler-dog relationship you see.''

She turned and beckoned toward a far door and three people came through it. Trotting at the left side of each was a dog.

"This is Jennifer. Her dog is an American Eskimo, commonly known as an Eskimo spitz...."

Dane was fascinated. The spitz was a midsize, fluffy white dog. The other two dogs were a German shepherd dog and a small black Skye terrier whose long hair was combed and tied at its ears with red ribbon. As Annie explained what the handlers were doing, all three dogs walked calmly on-lead at their handlers' sides and carried out the verbal commands they were given.

He couldn't believe Missy ever would be that well behaved. Even the little Skye terrier, whom Annie explained had just completed Basic, was a model of decorum compared to Dane's bouncy pet.

The dogs finished their demonstration. Even when the group applauded, not one of the dogs barked. As handlers and dogs filed off the floor, Dane was sorry to see the demonstration end. Not only had he genuinely enjoyed watching the dogs in action, he'd been able to observe Annie. Her eyes glowed as she spoke of the dogs, her body language was relaxed and confident and her piquant face radiated enthusiasm. It was quite a contrast to the reserved, wary woman he'd met three weeks ago.

"...now you can meet my dog."

With a start, Dane realized the demonstration wasn't over. Annie went to the far door, turned and faced the group, and, as if by magic, a large black dog appeared and sat at her side.

Dane couldn't take his gaze off the dog.

Sure, Missy was big. But floppy, ungainly and full of puppy friendliness. This creature had a squared-off, jowly face and a powerful, muscled body that would have done a prizefighter proud. This dog looked as if it could tear a person's face off without giving it a second thought.

"This is Evans' Ebony Rescuer, Ebony for short," Annie said. "Ebony is a three-year-old female Rottweiler. Rotties are descended from the dogs that herded the cattle for the Roman army."

"Will you show us what she can do?" This was from a woman in the front row.

Annie smiled. "I'd love to."

As she turned and asked the handlers to assist her in moving some equipment into place, Dane shook his head slowly. Whoa. The impact of that smile had caught him squarely in the solar plexus. She was gorgeous.

Then she turned to the black dog, who was lying near the door where she'd left her.

"Ebony, heel."

Immediately the dog sprang up and crossed to her in quick, eager steps, taking a sitting position at her left side.

Dane was impressed. Ebony's eyes were on Annie's face, her entire attention focused on her. She started forward, and so did the dog, still watching her face.

How long had it taken to create that kind of harmony, that perfectly attuned awareness that was obvious between the woman and the dog? She'd said obedience training demanded a lot of time. Judging from the depths of devotion shining in the animal's eyes, Dane could see she was a person who was able to give her dog that time.... What would it take to get her to focus that kind of attention on a man?

As she began the demonstration, he forced himself to quit thinking about Annie Evans on a personal level, and turned his attention to the floor. As he did, the scene before him grew more and more amazing.

Annie ran the Rottweiler through a series of increasingly complex exercises that involved a number of types of equipment. In the course of the demonstration, Ebony responded to about thirty different verbal commands before ending by retrieving a specific glove that carried Annie's scent out of a group of several others.

The woman next to him murmured, "Wow!" and he nodded in agreement.

Annie was thanking them all for attending and giving them last-minute reminders to be sure their dogs were brought on six-foot leads next week. He badly wanted to talk to her, but the moment she finished speaking, at least half the people in the room descended on her with questions. Reluctantly, he went out to the parking lot, wondering whether she'd accept if he asked her out on a date.

God, he hated the thought of getting back into the dating scene. Did women realize how stressful dating was for a man? How much courage it took to ask a woman out?

He'd done very little real dating in the two years since his divorce was final. The few times he'd been with a woman had been more of the scratching-amutual-itch date than the meeting-of-the-minds variety. In fact, *date* was a strong word for the kind of encounters he'd had in recent years.

But now, he found himself wanting Annie in more ways than merely the physical, though he certainly didn't discount that. He wanted to hear her voice, to know her dreams, to learn what was important in her life.

Unfortunately, he wasn't at all sure she was interested in him the same way.

The next day was a Thursday. Dane had just finished a conference call with two other bankers who were participating in negotiating a multimillion-dollar loan package for a local school complex when his secretary buzzed him.

"Mr. Patrick Murphy is on the line for you."

Dane's pulse speeded up a bit. Annie's brother. Picking up the line, he said, "Patrick. What can I do for you?"

Patrick's hearty laugh boomed on the other end. "How about a million or two? I've been thinking about this nice little trip to the Caribbean and I could probably manage it on that."

"One would hope," Dane returned dryly. "I might be able to swing that if you have room to take along a banker who'd be out of work."

Patrick laughed again. "I guess I'd better forget it. I couldn't ask you to risk your job, but there's a request that I don't think will get you in trouble. Annie and I are having a little barbecue Saturday and we'd like you to join us."

"Sounds good. I'm free Saturday." He fought to keep the elation out of his voice. In two days, he'd have an opportunity to see her again.

"Great! We'll be getting started around seven."

"Seven it is. What can I bring?"

"Nothing. Just bring yourself."

Dane hung up the phone a moment later, erasing his wide grin just as his secretary walked into the room. He was going to see her again, and he hadn't even had to call her for a date!

The doorbell's imperious summons rang again and Annie pulled open the heavy door. She'd been greeting guests by the dozens as she plastered another social smile in place. As she registered the wall of broad masculine chest covered in a blue knit shirt standing on her doormat, she had to force the words from a suddenly dry throat. "Welcome to the party."

"Thank you."

"Please come in."

Her foyer was immediately too small, lacking in oxygen. She dragged her gaze upward, but the moment she met piercing blue eyes, she knew she'd made a mistake. Those eyes were compelling, far too beautiful and thickly lashed for any man to own. Dane. Her new neighbor. Her client. She'd been aware of him in the audience at orientation the other night, aware of every move he'd made around the big training room afterward.

Not that she'd wanted to be. But something about the man pulled at her consciousness as if she were a metal filing and he the magnet. Suddenly, she realized she was blocking the hallway. Flushing, she stepped back, leaving plenty of room for him to pass.

Despite her care, he brushed by her as he stepped into the foyer, and she took in a deep gasp of air as the contact point where his thick arm brushed her shoulder sizzled. This close, she was even more acutely aware of how big the man was. Nick had been tall, and Patrick was over six feet, but Dane easily topped them both. His shoulders were broad, and even though the short sleeves of his shirt were loose, they didn't disguise the bulge of powerful muscle beneath.

He was smiling down at her, his eyes warm and his black curls straggling across his forehead. He extended a brown paper sack. "Patrick wouldn't let me contribute, but I brought a small token of my thanks. I haven't had much time to socialize yet, so this was a welcome invitation."

"Thank you." She felt tongue-tied and awkward as she took the bag from his and drew out the bottle. Her eyes widened as she took in the expensive label on the bottle of wine. Either the man knew his vintages or the clerk at the store had been awfully helpful. She glanced at him again, then away quickly, needing space more than she needed to breathe. "The party's out back. Follow me."

As she led the way down the hall, she was supremely aware of his large presence behind her. She should be making small talk, social patter to smooth over the awkward silence. But she'd never been good at that. It was one of the regrets she'd lived with since Nick's death.

Besides, with Dane there was some additional inhibitor catching at her tongue. She felt jumpy, as if she were in touch with a mild electrical field around him. Dane's eyes seemed to see too much, penetrating the indifference with which she'd cloaked herself in the past three years. When she looked at him, she felt an instant tug of attraction, the first time since Nick's death that a man had caught her attention in any personal way.

And it scared her to death.

# Two

In the kitchen, Annie set the wine on the counter and stepped back to the tray of raw vegetables she'd been preparing. "The party's right through that door." She nodded at the exit that led to the patio. "I have a few things to finish up in here."

But Dane didn't take the hint. "I really enjoyed the orientation session Wednesday night." He folded his tall frame into one of the chairs at the breakfast bar. "It was exciting to watch the trained dogs."

"Have you ever seen obedience work before?"

He shook his head. "We had a succession of mutts when I was growing up but I never saw any demonstrations of what a trained dog can do."

The way his mouth moved to form his words was fascinating. It stirred something deep in her belly— and she realized he had stopped speaking and was looking at her expectantly. What had they been talking about? Obedience. This was a topic she could manage if she just didn't think about *him*. "I remember the first time I ever saw an obedience demonstration. I was about fourteen," she said. "Patrick had just gotten his driver's license and he was itching to show off. Mom suggested we drive out to the county fairgrounds where there was a dog show being held and he leaped at the chance, even though it meant taking his younger sister along. Once we got there, I was hooked. They had to drag me away."

"Patrick mentioned that your family is from Chicago. Do your folks still live here?"

It was a personal question for such short acquaintance, a question that she might have found intrusive coming from someone else. But his blue eyes were warm on her face and she found herself answering before she thought about it. "My parents passed away while I was in college." She allowed her voice to reflect the love with which she always remembered them. "They were older when Patrick and I came along, and after mom died, my father just gave up. They were so happy together. I like to think that they're as happy now, together again."

"Was this your family home?"

She hesitated for a moment, the warmth between them forgotten under the onslaught of memory. "No. My husband and I bought this place after he established his law practice here in River Forest. As a child, I lived right in the city on Lake Shore Drive, in a high rise across from the lake."

Dane hesitated, too, and she had the impression he was weighing his words before he spoke. "Patrick told me you're a widow. Losing your husband must have been very difficult."

"It was." She bowed her head, fighting the threat of sudden tears. Just when she thought she had grief conquered, it sprang out to torment her once again. How could she still miss Nick so much and be attracted to another man? "I'll always owe Patrick a debt for the way he took over my life until I could get back on my feet. Even though I'll miss him terribly, I'm glad he's finally going to get on with his own life."

Dane looked quizzical. "Where's he going?"

She stared at him. "Didn't he tell you why we're having the barbecue?"

He shook his head.

"This is a farewell party of sorts. Patrick's moving into his own place."

One inky eyebrow quirked. "So you'll be living here alone?"

"No." She sighed. Though she'd never let on to Patrick, his leaving was a blow. She loved the big house but there was no way she could afford it on her own. "Don't tell my brother, but I'm going to have to find something a little less costly."

"What about an apartment?"

She shook her head definitely. "I want a house of my own. It'll be hard to replace this one, though. And Ebony would hate an apartment."

"I guess she would." Dane smiled. "I've never seen a dog so well trained. How long will it take me to get Missy to do those things?"

Annie almost laughed. "Several years. Don't put the cart before the horse. First you have to complete Basic. Your challenge is to strengthen the relationship between you and your animal and have the dog paying attention to you."

His eyebrows rose in a provocative smile. "Sounds like something I'd want in a woman, too."

She dropped her gaze to the tray of vegetables. *He was flirting with her!* Panic rose. She wasn't ready for this. The moment stretched between them as she cast around for something neutral to say, something that couldn't be misconstrued . . . and she realized she'd let the silence drag on too long.

Conversation dwindled after that. She felt all thumbs, trying to finish peeling the carrots. Though she didn't look at him again, she knew Dane was watching her.

The idea made her even more nervous, though she didn't quite know why. He'd been nothing more than courteous and friendly and a bit flirtatious . . . if you didn't count the silent message those eyes were broadcasting.

Maybe she was losing her grip. Maybe it was all in her imagination. She'd been alone so long that she was beginning to—

The sudden, sonorous peal of the doorbell startled her so badly she dropped the carrot peeler onto the counter with a loud clatter.

"I'll get that," she said shakily. Almost desperately, she turned from the counter. "Patrick's barbecuing in the backyard, right through that door."

After she'd ushered in another group of enthusiastic guests, she returned to finish her preparations in the kitchen. The black knife she'd been using lay on the counter and a memory rose, of Nick slicing his thumb with the same knife in the days right after their wedding.

God, she missed him. She wished for the anger she'd felt for a long time, but all she felt was weariness. Earlier in the week, she'd visited the cemetery, as she did about once a month, to trim the grass around Nick's headstone and tidy it up so that it didn't look so... alone.

As if the losses would be intertwined for all time, she remembered that he wasn't really alone, that Honey, their prize Rottweiler, was with him. The thought squeezed her heart painfully and a lump rose in her throat.

*Stop it, Anne Elizabeth. Just stop thinking about what you can't change.*

Blinking with fierce resolve, she looked out the wide window above the sink to where Patrick was gesturing wildly with a meat fork. He was in the middle of a group of people, obviously telling a story and enjoying himself immensely. His red hair gleamed in the bright sunlight. She was glad to see that he, at least, appeared to be happy now. The withdrawn, silent stranger who'd flown to her bedside in the hospital had been a shock, even through her grief. It had been months before she'd pried the truth out of him, learned that his marriage had ended the same week she became a widow.

Living together had been good for them both. She sighed, willing the grief back into its box. No woman could have asked for a more supportive, more loving brother in the past few hellish years. And she was going to miss his irrepressible silliness.

The back door opened and Annie hastily swiped at a tear that had escaped and was making a quick getaway down her cheek. She turned back to the dip she was mixing as her best friend, Jeanne Krynes, came over to drape herself across the counter beside Annie.

"Holy cow! Why didn't you tell me Adonis had moved into the neighborhood?" Jeanne faked a swoon, pressing her hand to her ample bosom.

"I presume you're referring to Dane?" She was proud that her voice was calm and even.

Jeanne grinned and smoothed a hand over the gleaming coil of blond hair swept out of the way. "None other. Did you get a look at the way he fills out those fine-fitting shorts?"

"Jeanne! Have you even met him yet?"

"I don't have to meet 'em to scope 'em," Jeanne said. "And I scoped your new neighbor. As I said, Adonis."

"Dane has black hair," Annie retorted. "Adonis is usually depicted as a blonde."

"Details, details." Jeanne waved a hand in the air. "He's drop-dead gorgeous and you know it." She sank onto a chair at the table and propped her long, tanned legs on the opposite seat. "Six foot two, eyes of blue," she warbled.

"Shh! He'll hear you." Annie could think of nothing worse than having Dane hear Jeanne extolling his virtues through the screen door. Especially when she privately agreed with her friend.

"So what if he hears me?" Jeanne swung her legs down and rose to lean her elbows on the counter. "Look me in the eye and tell me you don't think he's a fine-looking specimen of Number One Grade-A American Beefcake."

Annie felt the weight of her grief lessening under Jeanne's irresistible good humor. "Do I have to say it ten times?"

Jeanne's mouth quirked. "Without laughing."

They both chuckled.

Then Annie sobered. "I'm going to miss my brother."

Jeanne's brown eyes softened sympathetically, and she reached a hand over the counter to cover Annie's. "I know. If he wasn't such a pain, I'd tell him how wonderful he's been to give up three years of his life for you. But I guess it's time you got on with your life. Nick would have wanted you to." She sighed and squeezed Annie's fingers. "Is it getting any easier?"

Annie shrugged. "I guess." She knew what Jeanne wanted to hear. But she honestly couldn't say that she was glad she had come out of that operating room alive. She dropped her gaze to stare blindly at the tray of vegetables.

How did people do it—live on for a lifetime after losing the one they loved? How did they smile and act as if they genuinely enjoyed the warmth of a spring day? How did they laugh at jokes, or keep from screaming at the memories that sprung, unexpected, from around every corner?

It was true she'd learned to live with her grief. But every day was a struggle.

Shaking off the tears that threatened, Annie dredged up a smile for Jeanne. Squaring her shoulders, she picked up the vegetable tray. "Hold the door for me?"

Dane took the platter of barbecued chicken from Patrick and headed for the glass-topped table beneath the yellow umbrella. It was heavily laden with food, far more than the several dozen people scattered around the pool could consume.

He was happy to have an excuse to get away from two of the unattached females Patrick had invited. Both were the kind of good-time party girls who pursued a man at the slightest sign of interest. He knew the type well—and avoided it like the plague. The next wife he took was going to be a one-man woman.

As he hunted for a place to set down the meat, the back door opened. Annie came out, followed by her friend, Jeanne, the statuesque blonde to whom Patrick had introduced him earlier. She was married to Joe Krynes, who was frolicking in the pool with their two toddlers.

He envied Joe those kids. He'd wanted to start a family right away when he'd married Amanda, but she'd wanted some time...which eventually turned into a flat refusal to consider having a baby. Ever. Period.

At least, not *his* baby.

As he cut off the painful memories, his determination firmed. He fully intended to find a wife again someday and have that family. But he was smarter now. He didn't have to give his heart to get what he wanted, and he promised himself he'd never let a woman take him for a ride again.

His gaze was drawn to the man coming out of the pool with a child on each arm. He'd learned from Patrick that Joe Krynes had shared a law practice in Oak Park with Annie's husband. Joe smiled at the women approaching from the house.

The contrast between the two was striking. Annie was small, with her long copper braid and big blue eyes whose wary expression shouted, "Keep away!" Jeanne was much taller, a blonde with sparkling, naughty eyes of spaniel-brown. She offered him a come-hither smile as they neared. "Gimme a hand, handsome, and we'll rearrange this table to make some space."

He smiled back, aware of the open appreciation in Jeanne's gaze. Only a happily married woman could be that cheerfully lecherous. He wished Annie would look at him like that, he thought as he moved to take the tray of vegetables from her. "Where do you want these?"

Annie gave him a small, lukewarm smile as she surrendered the tray. Her head wagged once in the direction of the second patio table that held other picnic necessities. "Right over there would be fine."

She couldn't make it any clearer if she wrote it on her forehead, he thought as everyone came to the tables and Patrick brought over the chicken he'd finished grilling. Annie Evans wasn't thrilled about having him here tonight, and she definitely wasn't interested in flirting with him. She'd cut him dead when he'd dared to tease her earlier in the kitchen. As far as she was concerned, he was just part of the furniture.

Trouble was, he was beginning to think he was going to have to satisfy this yen he'd developed for her. It was becoming a matter of pride to get her to notice him as a man.

But when his gaze sought her again, she was hurrying over to Patrick, who was beckoning. One of the male guests stood beside Patrick, and after what looked like a few hearty comments, Annie's brother went back to the grill and left her alone with the guest. Though Dane couldn't hear what they were saying, it was obvious they were exchanging pleasantries.

He thought about joining them, about making sure the guy didn't hit on her, but before he could make up his mind, she drifted away again. The man looked mildly chagrined as he watched her retreat, and Dane struggled not to let his satisfaction show. Apparently, her aversion to guests wasn't restricted to him.

When everyone had gotten a plate, Dane looked around for an empty seat. There was one beside Annie and he made for it just in time to preempt another man from achieving the same goal.

"Sorry," Dane said blandly. He turned in Annie's direction, seeking a topic he knew would draw her out. "Do you look forward to the beginning of each new class you teach, or does it get boring after a while?"

She tilted her head consideringly. As she did, her long braid slipped to the side and he had to clamp down—hard—to resist the urge to wrap his fingers around the thick rope of hair and feel its texture, heft its weight . . . pull her closer.

"Obedience classes never bore me," she said.

Dane jerked his attention away from her hair to focus on the blue gaze she was directing his way. "Why not?"

"Each new group of dogs is exciting to watch as they learn to follow commands. I imagine it's a lot like teaching people. No two students are alike. In my case, that's even more true since the students come in handler/dog pairs. No two handlers work a dog in the same manner. It always fascinates me to watch the developing relationship between an owner and his dog as they interact."

Dane gave her a sideways grin. "Or the lack of it."

She didn't allow her lips to tilt up at the corners. "You seem to have little faith in my ability to help you to learn to manage your dog."

He choked on a piece of Patrick's excellent chicken. "No, that's not it at all." Hell! He didn't want her thinking he was going to be a thorn in her side throughout the lessons. "It's just that my dog is so . . . bouncy . . . that I can't imagine she's going to respond very well to training."

She did smile this time, and his pulse rate accelerated as deep dimples flashed in her perfectly rounded cheeks. "You'll be surprised."

Silence fell.

What else could he talk about that might interest her? She sat beside him, looking small and fragile and deliciously cool in her pale yellow shorts and striped sleeveless top, but she appeared completely unaware of his interest. He couldn't imagine how she could be so oblivious, when he felt like a radiator on the high setting, just from sitting next to her. Her blouse was a sheer fabric and he could see a hint of lace beneath...for such a small woman, her breasts looked surprisingly full. Suddenly, he noticed that Jeanne Krynes was grinning at him from across the circle of chairs and he wrenched his gaze away, feeling guilty color come into his face. Talk. He needed to find something to talk to Annie about....

"Patrick conscripted me to help with moving day."

Annie looked at him and smiled sympathetically. "Poor you. I bet he didn't tell you about his rock collection, did he?"

He made himself smile in return. "No. And I've just moved in, so I won't need him to return the favor, either." He remembered what she said about looking for another home. "I can see why you love this place. Was the pool in when you bought the house?" The shadow that slipped into her blue eyes was the same one he'd seen earlier when she talked about her husband, and he couldn't help wondering how it would feel to have a woman love him like that. "No," she said quietly. "The pool was a later addition."

"Your idea?"

"My husband's." Her eyes were blank again, as if she'd turned inward, denying him access to the woman behind the defenses. "Nick and I bought this house seven years ago, right after he and Jeanne's husband, Joe, opened their law offices."

He wanted to question her further—hell, he wanted to know everything there was to know about her! But he was afraid that if he pushed her, she'd only retreat farther into that polite coolness she used so effectively.

"An-nie. Hold me?"

Before Annie could respond, the little Krynes girl clambered into her lap. Dane watched curiously as a spasm of—pain?—discomfort of some kind, darkened her blue eyes for an instant before she smiled down at the tiny blonde. What went on in her head? She was an enigma, a mystery, and he wanted to solve the riddle of her reserve.

After the meal, nearly everyone sat around the pool or swam. Annie did neither. Instead, she brought her dog out of the house. Rather than rejoining the party, she wandered down to the far side of the yard, where Dane could see her examining a bright bank of summer flowers.

He grabbed his towel and dried off, then donned his T-shirt and joined her.

Ebony leaped high into the air for the Frisbee Annie tossed. As Dane approached, the dog came trotting back to her, leaning heavily against Annie's legs as she relinquished the Frisbee to her mistress.

He watched as Annie patted Ebony, irresistibly drawn by her pink cheeks and sparkling eyes. He bent and stroked the wide head, chuckling when the Rottweiler's broad backside wriggled back and forth in delight. How could he have thought this dog looked menacing? "You're a big old friendly fool," he said, fondling Ebony's ears and allowing the wide tongue to bathe his hand.

"Not always," Annie said. "She has a side you haven't seen here today."

"Is she trained to protect you?"

"I've had a temperament evaluation done on her and she passed. That means she acted aggressive in appropriate situations, and I have no doubt she'd defend me if anyone tried to harm me."

"She's not trained to attack?"

"No." She shook her head definitely. "I've never had a dog trained to attack. It's a big responsibility to have an animal that's a weapon."

Over Annie's shoulder, Dane could see Jeanne and Patrick cleaning up the remains of the meal. He would help in a moment, but he couldn't resist continuing the discussion while she was so open and receptive.

"Have you had other Rottweilers?"

Annie froze for a moment. She shook her head once, and her throat worked, but nothing came out. Tears sprang into her eyes.

*What the hell had he said?*

Dane felt as if his gaze were glued to hers. The horrifying sear of sadness in her eyes made him wish he could swallow his tongue; he was staggered by the depth of the pain he was witnessing. Despite what he knew of her past, he'd half suspected her reserve was deliberate, a teasing test of wills that he was expected to overcome. But he couldn't have been more wrong. The woman behind those mental walls lived in a hell he hadn't imagined.

Impulsively, he put out his hand, touching her lightly on the elbow. "I'm sorry. Don't answer if it's painful." He looked away from her to give her a chance to compose herself, and gazed across the pool where Joe was down on his hands and knees giving young Mindy a horsey ride. Beside him, he felt, sensed, her drawing in a deep breath, then letting it out in a controlled sigh.

"It's all right," she said quietly.

There was a long silence between them that he didn't try to bridge. What could he say? All he knew was that it most certainly wasn't all right. And that he hated being the cause of her pain.

Finally, he bent down one final time and ran his palm over Ebony's broad head. He risked a glance at Annie but she was staring into a past he couldn't share, reliving events at which he could only guess. The kindest thing he could do for her would be to leave.

But as he straightened and opened his mouth to thank her for the barbecue, she said, "I had another Rottweiler. Before Ebony. Honey earned titles in both conformation and obedience. We were coming home from an indoor show when a tractor-trailer jack-knifed just ahead of us. Nick, my husband, couldn't avoid it."

Dane froze for a second. Ugly, graphic pictures rose in his mind and he had to force himself not to reach out and hug her to him, to cut off the compulsive flow of words with compassion before she made him feel her pain again.

"Honey and Nick both died." She sighed and her breath caught. "I'm sorry. I rarely talk much about my loss. I feel like I've done nothing but dump on you all day."

"I don't mind." He stroked the dog again, then surprised himself by taking her hand. "Annie, I'd like to see you again. Would you have dinner with me next Saturday evening?"

The inspiration was out of his mouth before it was fully into his head, but the moment he heard himself speak, it hit him that he wanted her to say yes more than he'd wanted anything in a long time. He kept his gaze on hers, willing her to agree.

She was silent for an interminable moment and he braced himself for rejection. Hell, that should be no big deal. He was used to it.

"I'd like that," she said slowly. "But I have to warn you, I'm out of practice at dating."

"That's all right." Relief spread through him like a slow-moving river across a floodplain, so wide and deep that he felt limp beneath the weight of it. He knew a fierce satisfaction but quickly masked it. If she knew how badly he wanted her, she'd never set foot outside her door with him. Calmly, he said, "We'll be out of practice together."

"I find it hard to believe that you don't date much." Her voice was high and breathless and he realized he still held her hand, stroking his thumb idly across her palm. Glancing at her face, he saw hectic color spreading across her cheeks as she discreetly tugged at her hand.

Slowly, enjoying the flustered squeak she gave, he raised her hand to his lips and pressed a lingering kiss against the soft, warm skin. "I haven't had the urge to date much since my divorce. Until now."

* * *

The Basic Obedience class began at six o'clock on Thursday night.

It was just like any other class, Annie lectured herself. There was no reason to have butterflies battling their way out of cocoons in her stomach, no reason at all. It was probably something she'd eaten. She'd grabbed a quick sandwich from the deli down the street after the four o'clock Puppy Kindergarten class—maybe the tuna had been on the edge of turning. There couldn't be any other cause for this jittery feeling.

As the students began filing into the room with their dogs, Annie assessed each animal as she greeted everyone at the door. The Lab puppy was going to be a handful—he was a very playful nine months. The Dalmatian was the one in charge of his master, a relationship she hoped to be able to turn around by the end of the eight-week session. The German shepherd dog was just like all others of his breed, strong-willed and tuned in to one person and the shelty was so submissive, she bet he'd make a puddle on the floor the first few times he was corrected—

And the blue eyes gazing down into hers drove every coherent thought from her head. Had Dane grown more handsome? She knew it couldn't be, but in the four days since she'd seen him last, she'd swear his jaw had gotten squarer, his eyes more commanding, his lips more firmly chiseled. A lock of black hair fell onto his forehead in an irresistible curl. Deep slashes of dimple creased his cheeks as he flashed her a grin that revealed perfect white teeth.

He was breathtaking. *And she had a date with him on Saturday.* She must be out of her mind. No woman could be immune to that charm, could she?

Of course not. She'd noticed that every woman at the barbecue had turned up the voltage on her smile when Dane arrived. They'd have been more than happy to entertain him if he'd been receptive to their cleavage and their conversation.

A short, happy bark snapped her back to her senses and she smiled a little as she reached out to pat the Doberman straining to be noticed at Dane's side.

"Hello," she offered quietly, willing her voice to be normal. He might be good to look at, but he was just a man. Just a student, whom she happened to know personally. She should be relieved that she'd finally noticed an attractive man.

"Hi." His voice was as deep as she remembered. "Missy's raring for action. This should be interesting."

"It should be *educational,*" she replied. Unsure of what to say to him, she turned her attention to the dog, lavishly petting Missy before sending them in to join the rest of the group.

The class went well, despite her awareness of the black-haired man with the black dog.

As formal instruction hour ended, she moved around the circle of dogs, handing each owner an instruction review page. For a few, she made personal notes. Then she dismissed the class. Although her classes were an hour long, she always scheduled a half hour to allow for questions afterward, and tonight was no exception. Twenty minutes later, as her Novice class began to straggle in, she was just finishing with the last of the Basic students.

Dane had been standing near the back of the group during the question period. She was aware of his patient presence, aware of the blonde with the apricot miniature poodle who'd zeroed in on him as soon as the class ended. They appeared to have struck up a light and easy conversation and she could have hated the woman for that. She forced herself not to glance in his direction, to attend to the students asking earnest questions about training techniques.

Finally, there was no one else left. She offered Dane and the blonde what she hoped was a neutral smile. "Any questions before you leave?"

"No. I'm anxious to get started." Dane shifted a step closer, keeping his Doberman on a tight lead. "I'll pick you up about seven on Saturday, if that suits you."

She could see the blonde's ears perk up as smartly as her poodle's. Her face felt as if it were about to catch fire, and she willed herself to relax. *It's just a date. Everyone does it.* "Seven would be fine," she managed to say. "What should I wear?"

A strange light flared in his eyes for an instant. Then she thought she must have been mistaken because his voice was perfectly level and normal when he spoke. "I'll be wearing a tie, if that helps."

Dressy. She nodded.

There was an awkward pause then, and he finally said, "I'll see you Saturday."

"See you Saturday," she echoed. Saturday. Only two days away. A part of her dreaded the mere

thought of dating. Another part was responsible for
the shaky feeling that weakened her knees every time
Dane walked into a room, and it was that part of her
that could barely wait until Saturday to be near him
again.

# Three

Dane parked his white sports car in the circular driveway in front of Annie and Patrick's house, admiring the long, elegant lines of the Prairie-style home. As he knocked on the door, he remembered the way she'd nearly stammered with nerves on Thursday evening. He must be crazy to be wooing a cautious, skittish beauty like Annie. Only a certified nut case would take on such an impossible task.

He'd always enjoyed a challenge.

The door opened then and he snapped to attention. He'd never seen her in a dress, and if he'd thought she was beautiful before, now she looked ... well, ravishing was the only word he could come up with. And it was a fair approximation of what he would like to do with her, too. She'd worn her hair up, in an elegant twist that lent a classical beauty to her features. The dress she had chosen to wear caressed every one of her curves as if it had been painted on. Simply styled, it had a slim skirt with a wide belt topped by some kind of interesting bodice that wrapped across her breasts with no visible means of closure.

"Hi!" she said.

Her voice was animated and he was surprised by her high spirits. Then, as he looked closer, he realized the high spirits were nerves. Her smile was brittle and her eyes were too bright...she looked terrified, but trying hard to cover it.

"Hello." He kept his voice low and calm, hoping to reassure her, though his fingers itched to trace the neckline of that dress, to find out what, if anything, was holding the wrapped bodice together. "You look lovely."

"Thank you." Now her voice was a mere whisper. He wondered if she was regretting her decision to have dinner with him. He certainly didn't.

No, indeed. The dress made him long to touch. To explore that bodice, to slide his palms over the material draping her hips and thighs until he'd created a need neither one of them could resist.

And then what?

He'd very carefully avoided thinking of what might occur after he'd slaked this thirst he'd developed for Annie Evans. But now faced with that vulnerable, almost terrified look frozen on her pretty face, he knew this wasn't going to be as simple as he'd first imagined. Annie wasn't the type of woman to amuse himself with casually after he conquered. Nor was that all he wanted, if he were honest with himself.

When he'd first seen her, realized that she wasn't just another woman looking for a good time, he'd been seized by a compelling urge to overcome her reservations, an almost primitive conquest instinct that he suspected was closely tied to her seeming indifference to him. The thrill of the chase, perhaps?

Perhaps. But now he wanted more from Annie than just the challenge of getting into her bed. How much more...? Well, he wasn't sure he knew the answer to that. *Yet.*

A loud masculine clearing of the throat recalled him to the present. He realized he'd been staring at Annie until she was blushing. Patrick, who'd just entered the room, was glaring at him like an outraged father.

Deliberately allowing his amusement to show, he said, "Calm down, Patrick. I'm not going to gobble up your sister." He never took his eyes from Annie as he said, "Even if she is the most beautiful woman in River Forest." Oops. Wrong thing to say. The compliment clearly unnerved her even more.

He smiled at her, trying to tell her with his gaze to relax and was gratified when she made an obvious effort to pull herself together.

"Would you care for a drink?" she asked him.

He made a show of checking his watch, although it was unnecessary. No way he was going to linger under Patrick's protective eye a second longer than he had to. "I think I'd better pass. Our reservations are downtown at seven-thirty."

"Where are you going?" Patrick asked.

When Dane named an exclusive restaurant that was known throughout the Chicago area for its French cuisine, Patrick whistled. Then his good humor reasserted itself. "I don't know if she's worth that much. I'd opt for fast food, myself."

Annie sniffed. "No wonder you have trouble keeping your dates around for the second outing."

"My choice." Patrick preened. "'Love 'em and leave 'em,' that's my motto."

Dane laughed as he took Annie's elbow and steered her toward the door. "Ever heard, 'The bigger they are, the harder they fall'? It applies to egos, too."

As he shut the door behind them, Annie was laughing, a sweet, silvery sound that warmed his heart.

It appeared that she had subdued her reservations as she said, "Good comeback. It's rare for somebody to best my brother once he's on a verbal roll." But her tone was affectionate.

"How long have you and Patrick lived together?" he asked.

She raised an eyebrow. "You mean this time?"

"How many times have there been?"

"Three, if you count growing up, when we had no choice." She smiled. "And believe me, growing up with Patrick was an experience no one could forget."

"I can imagine." His tone was dry. "So when were the second and third times?"

"The second time was in college. He went to the University of Wisconsin and I followed two years later. We decided to share an apartment...which also was something to remember," she added wryly. "He had so many girlfriends I felt like a secretary trying to keep his schedule straight. And the worst part was that none of them knew about the others."

Dane laughed. "I can picture Patrick juggling fifteen women. Were you the same with the men?"

"Was I—oh, no." The animation drained out of her voice. "I met Nick, my husband—only he wasn't my husband then, of course—my very first week on campus." She gave a soft, sad little laugh that touched something deep inside him he'd thought was gone forever. "We fell in love on our first date. We got married the week after I graduated."

"Fell in love?" He echoed her words, knowing his cynicism had to show. "You mean you were sexually attracted."

She looked taken aback and a blush crept up her neck to spill into her face. "Well, that, too, but the physical side of our relationship was only one of the reasons I loved Nick."

"There's no such thing as love." He beat back the momentary nostalgia her words had produced. Any memory he had of young love had been an illusion, nothing more than a sensual preoccupation he'd shared with Amanda. As always, the thought of her betrayal was more than he could deal with. "Love is a euphemism that people use to dress up sex. Especially when it's great sex."

Annie's face was red all over now and her arched eyebrows drew together. She studied him carefully, as if he were a broken-apart puzzle and she were the person determined to fit all the pieces together again. "I have to disagree," she said in a soft but inflexible tone. "Nick and I never... I was a virgin until our wedding night, so our decision to spend the rest of our lives together wasn't based on sex. It was based on love."

He was silent, noting with relief that they'd reached the car. This discussion was going to go nowhere fast. He opened her door without speaking again, closed it after she'd slipped into the passenger side and walked around to settle himself in the driver's seat. It wasn't until he'd reversed the car out of her driveway and was moving out of the neighborhood that he spoke again.

"So now you're living with Patrick for the third time. Will you be glad when he moves?" Selfishly, he wanted her to pull her attention back to him, away from the husband for whom she still seemed to care so much.

She didn't answer for a moment and he figured she was angry at his last statement. He glanced across at her, only to be struck by the beauty of her profile etched against the Indian-summer sky. "In some ways, I'll be glad," she said finally. "Patrick was living in New Mexico when I was widowed. He had just separated from his wife. He came home to pick up the pieces of me and has stayed for three years. I'll miss him, yes. But I've felt guilty for disrupting his life with my problems. He might be remarried and a father by now if it weren't for having to look after me. Each of us needs to get on with our own life again, so in that respect, I'm glad he's moving."

Thank God she'd let their moment of discord drop. "You're very lucky," he reflected loudly. "I never had any sisters or brothers. I'd kill for a close relationship like you two share." *Hell, I'd kill for a sibling even if we weren't close.*

"I've always thought growing up as an only child must be very lonely," she said.

"I wouldn't know." Now why had he said that?

"Why wouldn't you know?"

His cryptic comment clearly had confused her and he was sorry he'd said it. Over the years, he'd learned that if he had to talk about it, it was best to just say it and get it over with. "I was left on the doorsteps of a church parsonage as a newborn. The only thing I had with me was a note with my name on it. The social services people don't even know if Hamilton was intended as a last or middle name."

He'd heard her suck in a breath of dismay as he spoke. Glancing over at her, he said, "You don't have to feel sorry for me. I was raised in a series of very acceptable foster homes."

"I'm not feeling sorry for you. What I am feeling is a strong urge to get my hands around the neck of the woman who gave you away." Her normally placid voice was as fierce as he'd heard it yet, and he forced out a light laugh.

"I wouldn't expend that much energy on her. If she didn't want me, I'm probably lucky she put me where she did. I could have wound up in a trash can."

Her fists were still clenched in her lap, but she made an effort to respond to his tone. "I guess you have a point. You say you had foster parents?"

"Three sets. The families are all very special—it was simply an unfortunate series of happenings that prevented me from being raised by any one of them. For example, one of my foster fathers lost his job and had to move out of state to find work."

"Have you kept in touch with any of them?"

"Yeah, but it'll never be like having a family of my own. That's why I think you're lucky to have Patrick." He made an effort to lighten the conversation. "Even if he is ... rather unique."

"Patrick may be quirky, but he's very special," she said, smiling a little. "Our parents both died while I was in college. I don't know how I could have gone on after the accident without him."

Silence filled the car then, but this time it was a comfortable silence that lasted until they were off the expressway, heading down Michigan Avenue. They spoke easily on the way into Chicago. As he drove, Annie pointed out local landmarks that he should be sure to visit someday, including Orchestra Hall, where the Chicago Symphony Orchestra played, and the Art Institute of Chicago.

It occurred to him that he could ask her to come down here and sightsee with him tomorrow, but he didn't want to press too much, too soon. She'd been reluctant to accept one date initially—she might refuse another if she felt pressured. And he wasn't prepared to take that risk.

During dinner, he entertained her with stories of the co-workers he had just met, and she told him about some of her experiences training dogs. Driving home, though, she clammed up again and he could sense the tension in the air, perched between them as solidly as a wall. He suspected he knew what was bothering her.

This was a date. And dates usually ended with a kiss. Was she dreading it? Or could she be anticipating it as much as he was? She was so quiet and still that he couldn't tell.

Taking a chance, he reached over and squeezed her hand where it lay in her lap, then let his palm lay loosely atop hers.

"Thank you for tonight. Moving to a new city has its lonely moments," he said.

Annie concentrated on his words. She was hearing him, but nothing made sense except the feel of his hard, warm hand covering her own and the intimate way his long fingers lay against her thigh. She could feel the heat searing her through the flimsy fabric of the blue dress. Swallowing to relieve a suddenly dry throat, she tried her voice, "You're welcome."

His fingers tightened briefly around hers, then he released her hand abruptly, returning his own to the steering wheel to guide the car smoothly into her driveway. Annie glanced over at him across the confines of the car's red leather interior.

Dane was . . . quite a man. Attractive and sexy.

Too attractive. And far too sexy.

Dane tempted her to take risks with her safe, comfortable life-style. She wasn't interested in changing it. Was she? Her heart had swelled with pity—and something more—when he spoke of his past. He'd been hurt, though he'd never admit it. And he could hurt her. She knew he was dangerous; knew it as surely as she knew that he could make her care again. And she wasn't about to do that. Not when she'd seen it all turn to ashes once before. *No way,* she silently told the huge silhouette at her side. *No way am I going to care about you.*

She wondered who she was kidding.

His voice broke into her thoughts as he escorted her across the driveway, but he halted her with a hand under her elbow before she could precede him up the walk. She hadn't left a light on and the evening shadows made the night a dark, intimate canopy filled by their presence. "If I come by tomorrow evening when I walk Missy, would you like to walk along?"

She knew what she should say. *No.* But her lips refused to form the word. She wanted to see him again, to be with him and explore whatever was growing between them.

Placing his hands on her shoulders, Dane softened his tone as he gently rubbed small circles with his palms over the silky fabric. "Tonight wasn't so bad, was it? Am I mistaken in thinking you enjoyed yourself?"

She stared at the paisley-patterned silk tie directly in her line of vision. His wide shoulders towered above her head and the huge hands masterfully caressing her wreaked havoc with her thought processes. She raised her own hands to where he massaged the softly rounded shoulder joints, intending to stop him, but he forestalled her by linking her fingers with his and holding them clasped between their bodies. Close to panic at the thought that he might kiss her, afraid more of her own treacherous responses than of Dane, she tugged her fingers free, sighing in unconscious relief when he allowed her to back away a pace.

"N-no. Tonight was…very nice. Thank you for the meal." She made a production of tucking her clutch under her arm with both hands. "I suppose tomorrow will suit. I'll see you then." Abruptly she turned and almost ran up the flagstone walk to the front porch, tossing over her shoulder. "I can let myself in. 'Night."

Dane noted her flustered reaction to his touch. She was so damn cool and collected most of the time that he wasn't even sure she returned the attraction he felt. Amused at her hasty retreat, he stood in her driveway, listening to the staccato tap of her heels on the flagstones. When the light in the entryway of the stately old home flashed on, and the porchlight winked once, he slowly folded his length into the white sports car, wondering ruefully how the hell long it had been since he hadn't gotten so much as a kiss on a first date.

Dane hadn't told her what time he would be by on Sunday evening, but she usually saw him walking his dog around six. When the doorbell rang at five forty-five, she had just finished tying her leather sneakers but her hair, which she'd washed and left down to dry, was still flowing around her body.

"Oh, rats!" she said aloud, grabbing her brush and a huge plastic clip with teeth in it to confine her heavy mane of hair. Pounding down the wide front stairs, she yanked open the door in time to see him securing Missy's lead around one of her front porch pillars.

"Hi! I'm running late. I'll only be a minute. Come on in and make yourself at home." *Shut up, Annie, you're babbling*. She moved aside so that Dane could enter. Her quick perusal revealed long, muscular legs in navy shorts paired with a knit shirt. She assured herself that her pulse was racing from flying around

getting ready—*not* from ogling a man's legs. When a
moment passed and he failed to move into the house,
she looked at him quizzically.

"Was it something I said?"

Still standing in the open doorway, Dane slowly
shook his head like a man awakening from a hundred
years' sleep. His blue eyes were fixed on her unblink-
ingly as he ignored her query, smiling slightly. "Good
evening," he said almost reverently.

Then, before she realized what he was up to, he
clasped her elbow and turned her in a slow circle.
"I've never seen such hair," he murmured. "Have you
ever had it cut?"

"Just the occasional trim," she replied, bemused by
his intense interest. At the pressure of his hand, she
turned fully to face him again. Each movement made
the copper strands twist and shimmer with a life of
their own. Dane reached out slowly, pulling handfuls
of fiery tresses forward to cascade over her breasts.

"Amazing," he said. Then, in a tone a full octave
lower, he informed her gravely, "There's something we
overlooked last night."

"What?"

"This." Tilting her chin up with one gentle finger,
he bent his head and lightly touched his lips to hers.

Too shocked by the unexpected move to draw away,
Annie stood passively as his large hands tunneled under her hair to cradle her jaw. *No!* she thought wildly.
*I'm not ready for this!* When he teasingly flicked his
tongue across the closed line of her lips, she gasped,
unprepared for even the light, nibbling kiss. The air
seemed to thin. She couldn't draw enough breath,

couldn't even think about moving as he invaded personal space that had been inviolate for years.

She could feel the furnace of his big, hard body crowding closer to hers, and at the second brush of his heated tongue, an answering spark flared in her. An unexpected frisson of need shivered down through her body to center between her legs and she gasped, fearful of the blatant sexual pull he exerted so effortlessly. He brushed his mouth slowly across her parted lips twice more before slanting his head and settling his lips more fully against hers.

His teasing tongue slipped between her lips with her second gasp, and suddenly, fear evaporated under a blazing need to calm her fevered senses with whatever magic spell he could provide. Unable to resist the primal demands he called from her body, she softened, leaning forward to bring her body into contact with his fully aroused male one.

In a moment of electric stillness, Dane withdrew his mouth a hairbreadth and studied her upturned face. He must have recognized her total female submission, because he slid his hands boldly down her back, hauling her up against him and fastening his mouth on hers.

Annie stiffened at the suddenness of the deeply intimate move and made a choked sound. Part of her was still wary of the sensations he aroused. She tried to turn her head away, but he twined one hand through her loose tresses, thrusting his tongue into the moist recesses of her mouth, and she stopped resisting as her entire body began to move in counterpoint to that rhythmic penetration. Her soft breasts pushed against the rock-hard planes of his chest, and she didn't resist when he lifted her completely off the ground, clasping one hand to her rounded buttocks to fit her hips against the ridge of hardened flesh at his thighs.

After the moment of instinctive fear, the sensual demands he was making blotted out all but the need to assuage her own desires. She began to respond mindlessly to the erotic play of his tongue and the slow, deliberate rub of his aroused body over her woman's mound. Her nipples were hard pebbles under the chambray top, clamoring for more contact. She squirmed more fully against him, totally lost in the moment . . . until the door slammed resoundingly just behind them. *Her brother!*

Annie jolted, once again struggling to free herself from Dane's embrace, but he subdued her with that effortless strength, pushing her head against his chest and keeping his arms hard around her. What must Patrick be thinking? Her brother had a wide streak of protectiveness where she was concerned; she only hoped he wasn't going to feel it was his duty to—

A loud guffaw interrupted her train of thought.

"Don't look so fierce, Dane." When she turned to face her brother, Patrick's handsome face wore a broad grin. "Just because I caught my one and only baby sister—"

"Shut up, Patrick." Strands of her hair were clinging across the shoulders of Dane's short-sleeved shirt. It seemed easier to concentrate on removing them than it was to meet her brother's gaze.

"I mean, just because you two were in a clinch so tight a crowbar couldn't have pried you apart—"

"Shut up, Patrick," Annie repeated.

"What I can't figure out is how come a combustible combination like you guys hasn't gone right up in flames."

"Patrick!"

"It nearly did," Dane said, and the sound of his deep voice sent shivers chasing up her spine. She took a step away from him, and this time he let her go.

"Hey, don't let me interrupt anything." Patrick folded his arms and leaned against the doorframe as if he intended to stay and take notes.

"Out, you—you twerp." Annie advanced menacingly toward him, brandishing the brush she'd discovered she still held.

"All right, all right. I can see when I'm not wanted. I'll just slink on out to the kitchen and make my poor, lonely little self a sandwich. You two go ahead and . . . well, you were doing fine without my help!" He vanished through the swinging door to the kitchen as Annie's brush struck the wood where his head had been a moment earlier.

Annie pointed at an ivy-covered building with a discreet brass plaque beside the door. "Remember my friend Joe? That's his office."

They'd been walking for nearly thirty minutes and Dane figured they were well over a mile away from home, even at the leisurely pace they were keeping for the dog's sake. This was the second time they'd gone walking together in the week since The Kiss. The kiss he longed to repeat. He glanced at the place she indicated, then looked again. Closely.

The sign read, Evans and Krynes Associates, Attorneys-at-Law.

"This is the practice your husband and Joe established?" Stupid question. Of course it was.

Annie nodded. "Joe has taken on two new partners since ... since Nick died. I've told him he doesn't have to keep the name, but he wants to." She smiled, and there was a sad fondness in her face. "I guess it helps him."

Dane evaluated the soft undercurrents of grief in her voice. He wanted to learn more about her marriage, about her husband. He wanted to understand her, *needed* to understand her, but he was afraid she'd clam up if he questioned her. She retreated into silence faster than anyone he'd ever known.

In as casual a tone as he could manage, he said, "How long were you—how long did you have together?"

"We knew each other for four years before the wedding. We were married about three years. And he's been gone that long already." She sighed, and the sound quivered with emotion. "Sometimes I can't remember what he looked like, the sound of his voice. Sometimes I wonder why I had to be left."

"Don't." He wanted to reach for her hand, but each of them had a dog in heel position. "You can't ask those kinds of questions. It's futile. You have to accept that this is the way it happened. You have to go on. Not forget, but go on." Damn. Why had he brought this up? It was so clearly painful for her. And he had less than no notion how to comfort someone filled with the kind of grief she appeared to have all bottled up inside.

"I know you're right. And believe it or not, it's getting easier. The memories still hurt, but they're beginning to fade. You know what I regret the most, though?"

She glanced up at him, and he was surprised to see her delicate features harden.

"We wanted children. But we wanted to wait a few years until the law practice was solid." She shook her head. "Now he's gone and I'd give anything to have a child."

"I know exactly what you mean. It's the one thing I regret about my divorce. I might miss the chance to have kids of my own because I made the wrong choice in a wife." He knew his voice reflected his bitterness and frustration.

Annie was silent for a moment. Then she said, "But you have plenty of time. You'll meet someone new one of these days."

He hoped she was right. But he didn't want to tell her he was already methodically searching for the woman who would be a perfect mother to his children. In fact, he didn't want to talk about himself at all. "The same goes for you. There might be another man out there who will give you those kids you want."

"Uh-uh." She shook her head so vehemently, tendrils of copper curls pulled out of her braid. "I'm never going to love like that again. I doubt I'll ever remarry. And that hurts. Because I'd love children of my own."

He hadn't said anything about love. Yet he found himself resisting the picture she painted. "You might change your mind one of these days. You're what... thirty?"

"Almost."

"Twenty-nine years old. Ten more years could change a lot of things. You could meet someone tomorrow." But he hoped she wouldn't. Not until he'd figured out what it was about her that he felt so drawn to, not until they'd played out whatever scene he was sure they had to play out together.

To his surprise, his words seemed to help. She sniffed and her lips curved upward again. "You sound like Patrick. He's always telling me Nick would have wanted me to get my life together and meet other men."

"Would he have?"

She nodded. "Probably. Nick didn't have a selfish bone in his body. He wouldn't have wanted me to grieve."

"Tell me about him." The words startled him as much as they probably shocked her, but he found that he meant them.

She was silent and for a minute he feared he'd overstepped the boundaries of their friendship. Or whatever it was they were creating. He knew he wanted more, more than Annie was able to offer right now.

"Nick...where to start?" she mused aloud. "How do you take all that a person was and distill it into a few sentences?"

"Don't try," he said promptly. "Just let the memories flow. Don't organize them for my sake."

She took him literally. For the next twenty minutes, a torrent of words poured out of her. They were standing in her driveway again, finished their walk, when she closed her mouth with a snap, as if just realizing where she was.

"Wow. I can't believe I talked that whole time." She looked a little dazed. "Why didn't you tell me to shut up?"

"I didn't mind," Dane said gently. "You must have cared for him very much." It was true. Every word she'd spoken had been filled with love for her deceased husband. It reminded him of his own miserable marriage and how far short of his optimistic dreams it had fallen. All he could think was that Nick Evans had been the luckiest guy on earth, to have been loved like that.

"I did." Her voice was quiet and sober. "Sometimes I think I was very fortunate, to have had that kind of love in my life, even though it didn't last long. Some people look all their lives for it." She glanced at him. "Do you know what I mean?"

"No." He knew the stiffness that had invaded his body puzzled her from the way she was looking at him, but he couldn't prevent it. He gave a laugh that was intended to be offhand but came out sounding harsh and hurt all at the same time. "What is love, anyway? Just a fantasy. Most people settle for a lot less, even when they think they've found the real thing."

Annie's eyes were very blue, soft with sympathy. "Is that what happened to you? With your wife?"

"Amanda." He spoke through his teeth. "Her name was Amanda and I thought we loved each other. But I found out that what I called love was nothing more than pretty great sex. Isn't that what love boils down to when you take all the fancy words away?"

"Dane, I'm sorry you were hurt—"

"I wasn't hurt." He moved away from the compassionate hand she placed on his forearm. "I was *lucky*. If Amanda hadn't left, I'd still be worshiping the ground she walked on while she was looking for a better deal."

# Four

She must have been temporarily insane to agree to this. How could she have forgotten how she hated this kind of thing?

Annie glanced around the crowded room at the other people attending the cocktail party. The alcoholic beverages being guzzled like water, the too-bright smiles and the too-hearty laughter made her stomach churn and quiver. Everywhere she looked, people were greeting one another with effusive hugs and kisses that looked too intimate to be on display.

And it was nobody's fault but her own that she was here. She *had* been out of her mind when Dane had asked her to come with him to this party, too dazzled by his charm to realize exactly what she was agreeing to until it was too late.

He'd been diffident, offhand, as if he was afraid she was going to refuse. And the contrast between that and his usual commanding persona had been so intriguing, she hadn't thought about what he was asking her to do.

"Annie, I've been invited to a get-acquainted cocktail party by the president of the bank's board of directors. Would you be willing to attend with me? I know it won't be a lot of fun for you, but I'd really like to have you there."

She'd actually been pleased, she recalled. He knew so much about her work. It was the perfect opportunity to find out a little more about what he did at the bank.

Now, looking around the crowded room, she saw that no serious business discussion was going to take place here today. When these people partied, they made a mission of it. Dane appeared to fit right in, though she knew he'd only worked at the bank for a few weeks. He was soon swallowed up by a boisterous group of men and she scanned the room for a corner where she could sit undisturbed.

Ah, there. She shrank into the corner, hoping that if she was quiet no one would notice her. How could she have forgotten how bad she was at making small talk? At finding something—anything—to say to people with whom she had absolutely nothing in common. It had been one of the few things she regretted about her marriage to Nick. She was terrible at The Social Thing. *Incompetent, that's what you are. A social zero.* Though she could scarcely bear to admit it, in her secret heart she felt an element of relief that now she didn't have to suffer through the endless functions that lawyers and their spouses were constantly attending.

"Hey, Millicent, who was that hunk I saw you with the other night?" A young blonde with what looked like several layers of makeup winked at several of the others as a group of women drifted over and claimed the arrangement of seats near Annie. "He was . . . not to be forgot." She giggled at her own wit.

Millicent looked annoyed. "Shh. Sherry, I swear you have the biggest mouth east of the Mississippi." She tossed a lock of carefully curled ebony hair over her shoulder and smiled reminiscently. "He works in my office. We just went out for a drink after work."

"And Paul doesn't mind that?"

Millicent shrugged. "What Paul doesn't know can't hurt him."

"And who are you?"

Annie realized with a start that the speaker was looking straight at her. The woman, tall with mannishly cropped hair, had just joined the group of women.

Millicent waved a hand in her general direction. "She came with the new man."

"I thought Dane wasn't married," the tall woman said again, making no effort to introduce herself.

"He's not." Annie rose and forced herself to hold out a hand. "I'm Annie Evans, Dane's neighbor."

The woman regarded Annie's hand with a slight smile, then raised a lighted cigarette to her mouth and inhaled. "We don't get formal around here. I'm Charlene Jenkins."

"Charlene wasn't expecting you," Millicent said to Annie. "She was hoping she could get a little of that action tonight."

"Or at least get a jump start on the rest of us," Sherry offered with another giggle.

"Why don't you have a drink?" Charlene took Annie's shoulder and turned her toward the bar. "It'll loosen you up."

Annie dug in her heels, realizing that her distaste must have shown, but she was past caring. "I don't care for a drink, thank you."

Charlene stopped pushing at her shoulder and eyed her in an assessing manner. "Oh God, not another bore like our sweet hostess."

There seemed to be nothing to say in response. It might not be kind of Charlene to have pointed it out, but she *was* a bore. Annie gritted her teeth and kept the social smile plastered in place. These women were vulgar and rude. They made the unendurable small talk she'd always hated seem positively irresistible in comparison.

"Annie?"

She glanced in the direction of her name. Her hostess, Lilith, was beckoning. The diminutive silver-haired matron had been by far the most genteel lady she'd met since coming through the door and Annie hastened to the woman's side.

"Have you had a glass of punch and something from the buffet?" Lilith slipped an arm through hers and steered her to the far end of the house.

"Thank you." Annie took a deep breath, realizing how tense she'd been as her shoulders relaxed from their rigid pose. "I'd like something to drink. Nonalcoholic, please," she added.

Lilith smiled. "Alcohol does amazing things to people's sense of propriety, doesn't it?"

"Amazing." Annie made an effort to smile.

"You mustn't mind those women," Lilith offered. "They're a bunch of bored housewives with too much money and too little to do. They play fast and loose with their own husbands and anyone else they can find, and they were hoping Dane was available."

Annie shot her a wry grimace. "Did I look that distressed?"

"I've tolerated them at enough parties to know when they're bothering someone." Lilith's faded eyes twinkled. "Let's speak of something more pleasant, shall we? Do you work, dear?"

Annie nodded. She was so grateful for Lilith's rescue that it was a moment before she realized the question required an answer. "Yes. I own a canine training school."

"Dog training?" Lilith's eyes lit up. "I love dogs. When the children were at home, we always had at least one golden retriever around the house, but now that it's just Arnold and me, I've downsized. Would you like to see my new baby?"

Annie nodded, grateful for the familiar topic.

"And where do you two think you're escaping to?"

The man was tall, but his eyes twinkled with the same kindly lights that Lilith's did. Dane stood beside him, obviously waiting for the answer.

"Oh, Arnold, have you met Annie?"

As Lilith introduced her husband, Annie realized the affable-looking Arnold was Dane's boss.

"Annie's a dog trainer, Arnold. Imagine that! I'm taking her for a peek at the puppy."

Arnold chuckled. "Why don't you go along with them, Dane. That's the only way I can be sure Lilith will find her way back. She hates these get-togethers with a passion."

Lilith rolled her eyes. "Don't be rude, dear. Go and mingle with our guests."

As she led them down a hallway and into what was obviously a family room, Annie marveled over what she'd just heard. So Lilith didn't like these things, either? No one would ever guess. Maybe she could take some lessons from Lilith on the fine art of socializing. Then she wouldn't feel like a millstone around Dane's neck—

Whoa! That thought brought her up short. As Lilith showed off the Maltese puppy that weighed less than two pounds when its long white coat was soaking wet, Annie asked herself when she'd begun thinking about being around Dane long enough for her social prowess to matter?

Dane eased his big body onto a chair in Patrick's newly furnished dining room, strained muscles protesting. Annie hadn't been kidding about the rock collection.

He knew he'd be stiff tomorrow. When Patrick had asked him to help him move from Annie's to his new place, Dane hadn't known that in addition to the things at the house, Patrick also had several rooms of furniture in storage. It was just like Patrick to forget to mention that small detail.

Annie carried two plates, one piled high with pizza, which she set before him, and one with two slices, which she put down at her own place.

She must have caught something of his mood, because she smiled and asked, "Are you wiped out?"

"Not as much as I will be tomorrow," he said with a wry grin. "Your brother forgot to explain just how much stuff he had stashed away when he suckered me into helping with this project."

She looked both mischievous and sympathetic at the same time. "Patrick's good at getting people involved before they know what hit them. Is there anything I can do for you?"

Rubbing the back of his neck, he smiled tightly. He'd like to show her exactly what she could do, and his body rose to meet the occasion. Stamping down the need for her that ran like wildfire through his blood, he shook his head and pulled out the chair next to his. "Just sit down here and keep me company."

As she slipped into the seat, the sound of metal clanging against metal jarred his ears. Joe Krynes stood at one end of the table with his toddler son, J.J., who was banging a spoon against the side of a pan with great enthusiasm.

"Hear ye, hear ye," Joe intoned as he held the pan out of J.J.'s reach and handed the child to his wife. "Jeanne and I have an announcement."

Eyebrows went up around the room.

"Do we get any hints?" Patrick asked.

"Sure." Joe grinned. "I'll answer 'yes' or 'no' questions."

Patrick drummed his fingers against the table. "You're taking a vacation."

"No."

"You're buying a new house?" someone else asked.

"Nope." Joe's eyes twinkled.

"You're expecting another baby."

Joe was silent for a moment. "No," he said, "*I'm* not, but..."

"...Jeanne is!" finished the speaker. "Congratulations. How long do we have to wait to see the newest member of the Krynes family?"

Joe and Jeanne exchanged a warm, conspiratorial look that Dane silently envied. What would it be like to have that kind of closeness with another person?

"I haven't been to the doctor yet," Jeanne said, "but we figure the baby'll be here shortly after Easter."

Dane glanced at Annie, measuring her reaction to the announcement.

Her small face looked pinched and white but she made a valiant effort to smile. "Congratulations! Another wee one for me to cuddle."

"Jeanne's incubating *again?*" Patrick sounded mildly shocked. "Man, haven't you two figured out what causes that yet?"

Joe just grinned and smiled. "We already know."

God, he was jealous. A son and a daughter, and now they were expecting a third child. Dane wondered yet again how he could have misjudged Amanda so badly that he'd lost his chance at all this. It only hardened his determination not to make a similar mistake in the future.

Beside him, Annie was talking to J.J., who had moved into her lap when Jeanne left the room. She was playing finger games with the giggling toddler. Every time she stopped, J.J. shouted, "'Gain, Anntie, 'gain!"

Joe chuckled. "The kids call her Aunt Annie, but J.J. hasn't figure out that it's two words yet."

Dane looked at the happy toddler. The child grinned back at him with the assurance of someone who's never met with rejection. Experimentally, Dane poked a finger into the little boy's middle. J.J. squealed and giggled, squirming in Annie's lap. Annie watched the child fondly, but the sadness Dane had glimpsed before still lurked in her eyes.

She'd lost her husband before they could start a family and he knew she minded the loss—she'd told him so. These children probably reminded her of her own loneliness every time she saw them, reminded her that she might never have any of her own to love. From the look on her face, it was obvious that she liked children. How she must regret not having her own.

*She could have your child.*

The thought was so unexpected that he caught his breath. He glanced at Annie again from the corner of his eye, afraid she might somehow divine what he was thinking. What *was* he thinking, anyway? Sure, he was more attracted to Annie than he'd been to any woman since... since he couldn't remember when.

Now that the treacherous seed had been planted, he couldn't keep from furtively examining it over and over again. Annie would be a wonderful mother, he thought, watching her with the chubby toddler, and he already knew she longed for children of her own, so there would be no unpleasant changes of heart after the wedding. They were compatible, they were going to be great in bed together—

J.J.'s mother entered the room again and the child lurched off Annie's lap and went wobbling across the floor to Jeanne.

Dane turned to Annie. This hadn't been a date, exactly, but he hoped she'd let him take her home. He wanted to consolidate the ground he'd won when he'd kissed her the other day. She'd seemed remote and withdrawn after attending that stupid cocktail party with him the other night, and he'd forced himself to give her only a chaste peck on the forehead. Tonight was going to be different.

"Ready to go? It's been a big day and I have to work tomorrow. I can drop you off at your house if you like."

Annie's shoulders drooped as he helped her to her feet and she raised one hand to massage her forehead as if to ward off a headache. "That would be nice."

He couldn't stand to see her look so beaten. Stepping forward, he placed his hands at her waist and drew her to him, turning so that his back was to the rest of the room. "What's wrong?" he asked in a low voice. "Jeanne's news got you down?"

To his relief, she allowed herself to rest against his chest as he began to rub her back in small circles. She felt incredibly soft and warm beneath his hands and he was supremely conscious of the tips of her breasts brushing against him.

Her head dipped once in assent. "A little bit. It reminds me of what my life should have been like."

"It still can be." *You could marry me and have a whole houseful of babies.*

"I'm fine just as I am." But she didn't sound fine.

He could tell this wasn't the time to push her and he wasn't ready to blurt out any half-formed plans. "I couldn't agree more. You're perfect just the way you are." He'd been striving for a light, playful tone, but the words came out in a husky half whisper.

Annie slowly raised her head from his chest. Her eyes were wide, her gaze questioning. She had beautiful eyes. Tonight they were a soft, misty blue, fringed by lavish dark lashes that matched the shade of the braid trailing down her back, bumping the backs of his palms where they cradled her. What would she do if he kissed her? His gaze slid to her mouth, wide and appealing, measuring the sweet bow of the top and lingering over the full bottom lip. As he stared, her lips parted slightly and he became conscious of her breath rushing in and out, bathing him in warmth. His body stirred, pulsed, growing to fullness, and his hands tightened fractionally on her back as he fought not to pull her against him.

Behind them, someone laughed. Belatedly, he remembered that they were standing in a roomful of people. With a silent curse, he let her go. "Let's get out of here."

She seemed subdued on the short ride to her home. When he handed her out of the car, he wondered if she was going to slip away from him the way she had the first time he'd taken her out to dinner, but she allowed him to take her hand and lead her up the steps to her front door, where he turned to face her.

"Give me your key."

His voice was a low growl. It made her stomach jump in anticipation. She knew what he wanted, and she knew that tonight, if Dane kissed her, she wouldn't resist. She longed for his touch, ached for it, with every fiber of her being. She didn't understand or even like the way her body reacted to him, but just for tonight, she wasn't going to think about anything.

He took the key she dug out of her bag and unlocked her door, then handed her the key.

She slipped it into her pocket. "Thank you." The air practically quivered with tension; she wondered if he could possibly be unaware of how much she wanted to lose herself in him.

When she raised her gaze to his face, he wasn't smiling. Instead, his features looked as if they were graven in stone. Time seemed to stop for a long, breathless moment as he raised his hand, and she held her breath in suspense.

When his long fingers slid underneath the heavy fall of her hair and cupped the back of her neck, she sighed. Slowly, his gaze commanding hers, he drew her braid to one side, wrapping it around one lean palm.

Annie quivered in delight as his head slowly came down. It was always like this when he touched her; all her senses focused on the sensations aroused by his clever fingers and seeking lips.

He kissed her and kissed her, until her knees buckled and she was clinging to him. At last, he raised his head and his eyes glittered in the dark shadow of the porch. "When can I see you again?"

"I—I don't know." Her voice sounded breathless and weak, even to her. "I can't think when you're touching me."

Dane laughed, a deep, primitive sound of satisfaction. "Good." Slowly, he released her and stepped back a pace. "I'll call you tomorrow."

She nodded once, then slowly turned away to open the door. Just as she put her hand on the knob, she felt him step forward again. His warm lips touched the tender skin at her nape and she drew in a sharp breath, unprepared for the surge of longing that shot through her.

Standing perfectly still, her head bent, she closed her eyes in ecstasy as he trailed a lingering kiss around to nibble at the lobe of her ear. She swayed back against him and his large, capable hands clasped her hipbones, pulling her firmly into contact with his big, hard body. He was aroused; she could feel the telltale ridge of his manhood pressing intimately into the small of her back. As his tongue dipped into her ear before swirling in a leisurely manner around the delicate shell, she whimpered, unable to stem the small sound that rose unbidden from her throat.

The tiny noise seemed to break the spell that held them. Dane withdrew his hands from her hips. "Tell me to leave."

She expelled choked laughter. "Will it work?"

"Unless you want me in your bed tonight, you'd better hope so."

She turned to face him, suddenly unsure. Everything was happening so fast. What did she really know about Dane Hamilton? She was a widow. A woman who still compared every man she met to her husband. But she'd hardly thought of Nick since Dane had come into her life. Her thoughts were chaotic, strewn with conflicting feelings of longing and guilt, need and remorse.... "I'm not ready to ask you in," she said.

"I know." His voice was still deep and rough, but oddly soothing. "Go inside. Now. I'll call you."

He did call her, several times, although they didn't see much of each other in the next week. On Thursday night, he was the first student to arrive for class, simply because he couldn't wait any longer to see her.

"Hello." He stuck his head around the door of her office as he and Missy entered.

"Hi." The way her face lit up when she saw him was an encouraging sign. Did she want to be with him as badly as he wanted to see her again?

Unable to stop himself, though he knew anyone could walk through the door of the center at any moment, he stepped into the office and held out his hand.

Without a word, she placed her much smaller palm in his and rose. Dane gathered her to him, gasping as her soft curves pressed against him. He buried his face in her hair and inhaled deeply. "You smell sweet."

He felt a little laugh that bubbled up from inside her. "It must be the 'Eau de Dog' I applied this morning."

He smiled, rubbing his chin lightly along her temple. "You're slandering my sense of smell." Then he shifted back a fraction so that he could see her face. "Have you missed me?"

She hesitated and his stomach dropped to his toes. *This shouldn't be so important,* he lectured himself. Then she nodded, and immediately he felt as if he could sprout wings and fly.

But all he said was, "Good," in a voice deep with satisfaction. He hadn't intended to come in and kiss her first thing, but as he gazed at her, he knew he had to taste her again. Slowly he lowered his head.

Annie didn't make any move away from him. In fact, she rose on tiptoe to meet his descent. The moment their mouths met, he knew he'd been wrong to do this.

Wrong. Because moving away from her without being sated was going to be hell on earth.

He forced himself to go slowly when all he wanted was to plunge his tongue into her and demand a response. But Annie reminded him of a wary doe and he was afraid if he moved too fast, she'd bolt. So instead, he stealthily increased the intensity of the kiss as they stood locked together in her office, kissing her until he couldn't remember where he was or what had come before this moment.

When he'd initiated the kiss, his hands had settled at her waist. Now he carefully, easily, slipped them beneath the hem of the loose sweatshirt she wore until his fingertips rested against flesh. His tongue continued to master her mouth and while she was so fully his, he risked flattening his palms over the bare skin of her back, savoring the silky texture of her beneath his hands. Slowly he rubbed rhythmic circles that matched the cadence of their mouthplay, and with each circle he increased the scope of his reach by millimeters, until his thumbs were brushing the sides of her full breasts with each stroke. Still she didn't protest. The next time his thumb swept across the ripe mound beneath her shirt, he spread his hand wide, whisking his thumb directly over the taut, straining peak concealed by a thin layer of satiny fabric.

Annie jerked and gasped against his mouth. "No! Dane, wait." Frantically she stepped away from him, pulling at his hands.

A hollow click preceded the opening of the outside door, heralding the arrival of other students. He uttered a silent curse, holding her by the waist when she would have put the width of the small room between them. "Annie." He stood very still until she glanced at him. "Tell me why you stopped me."

Color rose in her cheeks. She looked around the office. "Not here. It's not . . . private."

He felt a primitive delight leap within him. "Did you dislike what we—what I did?"

She dropped her gaze and her color rose even higher. The pause was pregnant with anticipation. "No," she said in a stifled tone.

"Good." He pressed a quick, hard kiss onto her startled lips and released her before any inquisitive students came looking for her. "The next time I touch you, it will be someplace where we won't be disturbed."

Her eyes were dark and unsure as she stared back at him for a moment. Then, apparently deciding silence was the best defense, she got Ebony out of her training crate and left the room. He stayed in the office for a moment longer to get his unruly body under control so that he didn't embarrass Annie—or himself—in front of the class.

As the lesson commenced, only part of his mind was on working his dog. The other part watched Annie, assessing every move she made, wondering how long it would be until he could touch her again. He was determined to have her now that he knew how responsive she was, and that she wanted him, too.

Once again, the speculations that had been rolling around in his brain surfaced. Was Annie the kind of woman he wanted for a wife? He knew she wanted children, so there'd be no problem there. He found her company soothing, her gentle humor healing and her sweet responses to his touch so wildly erotic that just thinking about it produced an uncomfortable surge of excitement centered in his groin. Was that enough for marriage?

He was beginning to believe that it would have to be.

* * *

It seemed fate was conspiring to keep her from making any rash decisions. He had meetings. She had classes. The following weekend he had to drive to Peoria for a wedding…two weeks crawled by and she didn't see Dane except during obedience class.

She'd never minded the odd hours before, but having a job that demanded she work evenings and Saturdays when everyone else was off seemed to be a big disadvantage all of a sudden.

Annie shook her head as she knelt in the flower bed at the front of the house on Sunday evening checking her autumn annuals. It was probably just as well she hadn't been free. She was becoming much too obsessed with Dane Hamilton. Just because he had enough sexual charisma to melt her into a puddle at his feet didn't mean she should jump into bed with the man. Annoyed at herself, she yanked hard on a particularly stubborn weed and when it easily tore loose, landed square on her backside in the dirt with an inelegant curse.

"Who won?" The amused masculine voice coming from directly behind her didn't belong to Patrick. Her heart skipped a beat and her breathing became shallow as her body reacted to the presence of the man who'd been in her thoughts.

He was clearly struggling against an outright guffaw, and reluctantly seeing the humor in the picture she must have made, she craned her head around to stick her tongue out at him before she collapsed into laughter.

"Better be nice to me. I come bearing gifts," he said. Reaching into a white paper bag, he produced a sinfully delicious-looking banana split and two spoons.

"Oh, yum!" Annie's eyes widened in delight. "My hero! I absolutely love banana splits. Where'd you get this?"

Blue eyes twinkled at her reaction as he told her the name of a local dairy. "If you can tear yourself away from your flower beds—" here his smile dissolved into a chuckle "—we can share it."

Annie leaped up. Before she allowed herself to consider her actions and chicken out, she stretched up and kissed his cheek. Then, embarrassed by her forwardness, she led the way into the house.

Dane took one spoon and dug into the sundae, holding a tempting spoonful of ice cream right in front of her lips. "Open sesame."

Annie let him feed her the bite of sundae; it was an oddly intimate sensation. Her eyes clung to his for a long moment as she savored the cool treat. "I didn't expect to see you tonight."

"I got back into town early." He paused to wolf down a huge bite of ice cream. "Do you mind my stopping by? I'm sorry I didn't call first but I came on impulse." He flashed her a grin. "It's lucky you were home or I'd have had to eat this whole thing myself."

Annie couldn't help but return the smile as they divvied up the snack. When he turned on the charm, he was irresistible.

Who was she kidding? He was irresistible even when he wasn't trying to please. His raven hair gleamed, casually disordered by impatient fingers. Thick, arched dark brows nearly met above a blade-straight nose and strong chin, a chin that Annie knew could jut into a stubborn firmness. As she watched, his tongue slid out and smoothly swept the last particle of ice cream from the spoon. She couldn't suppress the surge of desire that shot through her body at his unconsciously erotic motion.

When Dane lifted his gaze from the empty container, she knew he could read naked need in her eyes. His eyes narrowed to mere slits of blue as he dropped the forgotten plastic to the table. One lean, blunt-tipped finger lifted. Slowly, he tilted up her chin and when she didn't protest or pull away, he pulled her closer and lowered his mouth to hers.

She kept her eyes open, locked on his, until the first contact. But when his lips touched her waiting mouth, she sucked in a small gasp of air, and her eyes drifted closed.

# Five

**D**ane surrendered himself to the sweet sensations of kissing Annie, ignoring the roaring rush of his body urging him to move faster, deeper, farther, and keeping it light and nonthreatening as he knew she needed it to be. He kissed her like that for longer than he thought he could stand, until she slipped slender arms around his neck and speared her fingers through his hair in a signal that she was as involved as he was. Not wanting to scare her, he slipped his own arms around her slim waist, pulling her out of her chair sideways across his lap without breaking the kiss.

He nibbled and played with her warm, soft lips, seeking her tongue. Hesitantly, it seemed, she allowed him to part her lips and touch the tip of his tongue to hers. The erotic sensation sent an electric quickening through him and he forced himself not to rub his aroused body against her like some inexperienced teenager. When he had enticed her into meeting him halfway, he sucked at her, pulling her tongue into his own mouth to continue the erotic foreplay.

Her hands clutched at his biceps. He told himself to take it slow, to go easy. But he felt as if his willpower was made of soft clay as his fingers reached out to stroke and pet the sweet mound of her breast as he had once before. Annie whimpered at the first shock of contact but she didn't pull away and he was encouraged to make bolder forays. As he continued to knead her breast, her fingers slid across his broad back, pressing him even closer. His thumb and forefinger skillfully pinched and rolled the tip of her swelling flesh through her dress and bra and she began to shift restlessly.

Experience had taught him to read female signals. "Easy, sweetheart," he whispered against her mouth as he slid his hand down her torso and slowly, sweetly stroked the vee between her legs. "Easy," he whispered again when her thighs clamped together on his hand and she moaned. He was perilously close to the edge of his own control, his heated sex throbbing rhythmically against her hip as they strained together, seeking a better fit for their bodies. Breaking contact with her mouth, he lifted his head to measure the distance to the hallway. Annie immediately transferred her attention to his neck, nipping the corded sinews along the side. He shuddered. God, she was driving him wild. Her little noises and soft body felt so good he knew he had to have her. But not here. Concentrating fiercely to resist her long enough to get her somewhere more private, he decided to carry her upstairs. He knew the stairwell was right in the front hallway.

He rose and lifted her into his arms all in one smooth motion. Striding into the hallway, he paused at the front door and locked it with one hand. The implications of that very final-sounding click obviously reverberated in Annie's ears; her eyes grew enormous as she registered his intent to stay.

"Your back will be sore tomorrow," she said, smiling.

He paused in the hallway. "You'll just have to help me find a position that won't strain it too much."

She buried her face in his neck to hide the blush he'd seen beginning to spread. "That's not what I meant!"

His chest heaved with laughter beneath her and he stopped at the bottom of the stairs. "I know." He was silent for a moment. "I want to stay with you tonight. Am I right in thinking that's what you want, too?"

Annie raised her head from his shoulder. He read hesitation in her face for a long, agonizing moment. Then she said softly, "This is what I want." In a rare display of courage that he knew must have cost her, she ran her hands into the silky thickness of his hair, pulling his head down and finding his lips with her own. Dane groaned, afraid he'd never be able to take this as slowly as he should, given her lack of recent experience.

He climbed the stairs in silence. When he reached the top, he hesitated, wondering which one was her room. Annie lifted one hand from where it lay against his stubbled jaw and pointed to the second doorway on the left. With three measured strides, he was in her bedroom.

Standing beside the bed, he released her legs, allowing her to slide down over his taut body until she touched the floor.

"Where's a light? I want to see you."

Obediently Annie snapped on the beruffled, feminine lamp on the table beside her bed. It was a small light, and its low illumination barely reached into the darkest corners of the room.

Still, it satisfied him. He reached past her and swept the covers back to the foot of her wide bed. "Such a big bed for one little body." What he really wanted to ask her was if her husband had shared this bed with her—he didn't know why, but the idea bothered him.

As if she sensed what he really wanted to know, she said, "Nick never slept in this bed. I didn't keep any of our furniture after he was killed."

Her tone was bleak and he was immediately sorry he'd reminded her of her past. Reaching for her, he cuddled her against him. The contact reignited fires that had been temporarily banked, and suddenly he couldn't wait any longer. Removing a small packet from his wallet, he tossed both onto the bedside table before bending to her. She lifted her chin to meet his descending mouth. The gentle pressure of his lips opened hers easily and he slid his tongue inside to explore the ridge of teeth, sucking persistently at her tongue until she followed his dancing retreat into the moist depths of his own mouth. He slid his arms down her back as he responded to the exciting foray her tongue so tentatively made. Then he boldly let his hands wander over her firmly rounded buttocks, lifting her until her feet dangled off the carpet and the hardened bulge of his arousal nestled in the vee at her thighs.

A wave of weakness swept over her and she melted bonelessly against him, assailed by intense physical sensations that she had never dreamed she could feel. Deep in her torso, an unaccustomed throbbing had her shifting against him, rubbing herself rhythmically over his hardness in a unconscious effort to alleviate the building tension within her. Dane shuddered, wildly thrusting his hips against her through the barrier of their clothing. She was more responsive than he had ever imagined in his most erotic dreams...and he'd been tormented by plenty of them since he'd met her. She had him ready as a stallion and he hadn't even gotten her clothes off yet. Sweat beaded his upper lip as he fought for control. More than he'd ever wanted anything in his life, he wanted to do this right for her. She was too fragile to be taken with anything less than the gentlest touch he could manage.

Summoning all his willpower, he released her soft curves, shuddering again as her ripe figure rubbed against him.

He smiled crookedly down at her, reading every nuance of her passion-dazed expression. "I don't want to hurry this," he told her. "We have all night." Smoothing his palms up her torso, he framed the generous weight of her breasts between his spread thumbs and forefingers. "I want to see these beautiful breasts.

I've been driving myself crazy imagining what they look like.''

Annie blushed and he smiled. How she could still do that after some of the erotic movements she had made was beyond him. It pointed, once again, to the extraordinary blend of innocence and sensuality that he was sure she didn't realize she possessed. He could see the rosy color spreading up her neck even in the dim light cast by the little lamp. His thumbs lifted to flick across her nipples for an instant and then he was sliding those knowing hands around to the back of her dress, smoothly releasing the zipper beneath the unbound mass of her hair. Stepping back a pace, he stood, breathing hard, just looking at her for a long moment. The strapless sundress was loose, but it had caught on the peaks of her upthrust breasts. He reached out and inserted one finger between the neckline of the dress and her silky skin, running it from the tip of one breast to the tip of its mate. Just that action made the dress fall away from her petite body, pooling around her ankles.

Dane sucked in an involuntary breath, standing as if turned to stone, staring at all her displayed beauty. She had worn no bra beneath the dress, and her sole garment now was a pair of tiny panties, which were cut so low that he could glimpse the beginnings of the copper curls covering her feminine mound. To his delight, her breasts were bigger than he had envisioned, round and full without sagging, topped by rosy-pink nipples that were tightly beaded. He already knew that she had a waist he could probably span with his hands. The one detail that his vivid imagination hadn't supplied was the creamy texture of her skin as it flared into smooth thighs kept slim and lightly muscled by hours of hard work. He could feel his heavy arousal rising to full attention, but he forced his mind off his own needs, correctly reading the embarrassment she was unable to hide.

"You have nothing to be ashamed of," he told her in a husky voice. "You are perfect."

Annie managed to find her voice, though she was conscious of the heat staining her cheeks as well as a very different type of heat curling insistently through her midsection. "No, I'm not," she objected. "I'm too small and my hair is the most awful shade—" She stopped abruptly as Dane reached out to cup the weight of one full breast in a tanned hand, reacting like a cat to the stimulating caress.

He watched her back arch as she unconsciously pushed herself against his hand. "You are not too small. Your breasts are generous and I can barely keep my hands from tearing the clips out of those glorious curls of yours when you wear your hair up. You turn me on so fast and so hard that I have trouble hiding it when we're in a public place. Now—" he took a deep breath "—will you help me undress?"

Tentatively, she moved her hands to the small buttons of his shirt. Although trembling with nerves, her slender fingers moved surely down the front of the garment, revealing an ever-widening strip of toasty skin lightly covered with silky black curls. As she neared the waistband of his pants, her hands slid inside the shirt, smoothing it off his sleekly muscled shoulders. Unable to resist, she slowly dipped her head to bury her nose in the cloud of curls, inhaling deeply. He smelled musky and excitingly masculine and she detected faint traces of his cologne. Nerves were forgotten as she was caught up in the sensual excitement he radiated. Rubbing her nose from side to side, she encountered a flat male nipple which rose to meet the gently circling tip of her pink tongue.

Eyes half-closed, awash in the sensations she was evoking, Dane watched her lightly trace his nipple with that teasing tongue for a moment before the pleasure threatened to cut short her explorations and his hands slid from bare hips to her shoulders to draw her a hairbreadth away from him. "No more," he commanded, and her eyes flew to his in confusion. Smiling in self-derision, he added, "I can't take it."

His hands left her shoulders to swiftly deal with the rest of his clothing. As he drew his slacks down over strong thighs, the evidence of his desire was clearly outlined by clinging navy briefs. Then he removed those, too, with an impatient sweep of his hand. He was bigger, more aroused, than Annie had known a man could be, and she quivered deep inside at the thought of joining with that magnificent frame in the act of total intimacy.

Dane mistook her long silence for fear. Drawing her into his arms, he feathered open-mouthed kisses along her jaw, down her neck, and finally to the crest of one sloping breast. "Don't worry, baby," he breathed against her skin. "We'll be a perfect fit."

Waves of excitement coursed through her as his lips suckled strongly at her. She could feel his satiny hardness brushing insistently against her belly, and her legs suddenly wouldn't hold her another second.

Sensing her capitulation, Dane moved to take swift advantage, scooping her up only to deposit her almost instantly on the mattress. Long fingers hooked in the tiny panties and pulled them off. The bed gave as he joined her, and Annie was conscious of the way his broad shoulders deleted her view of the room before his dark head came down and she closed her eyes. He kissed her deeply, repeatedly thrusting his tongue into the moist depths of her mouth as one skilled hand shaped the sensitive peak of her breast until she was whimpering and moving restlessly beneath him.

"What's the matter?" he crooned. "Let me make it better."

His words washed over her, but the exact meanings were lost; *she* was lost, drowning in the magic that his hard fingers were working on her flesh. As one calloused hand slid firmly down her stomach, combing through the crisp curls between her legs, she drew in a sharp breath. It was released in a thin cry as a dexterous finger probed the soft folds of the feminine rise, dipping and rubbing the small bud hidden there, sending fiery messages to every part of her body.

Annie responded totally to that knowing hand for uncounted minutes, trusting him without question, and her hips lifted repeatedly, legs shifting and spreading to invite a more complete possession.

Dane nearly succumbed to the need screaming at him to take her when he slipped his hand between her thighs. Her eyes were closed and her bright tresses spilled across the pillow as her head thrashed from side to side. She was slick with her own moisture and he knew he wouldn't hurt her if he took her now, but he wanted more. Holding back his own desire to lose himself in her writhing excitement, he carefully slid two fingers deep into her, continuing to stimulate her center with the butt of his hand. Her back arched and she gave a muted scream which he caught with his own mouth. As she peaked, ever-spreading waves of fulfillment lapped through her body, relaxing muscles held stiff and tense with desire.

He was nearly wild with the need to be inside her. Even as her body jerked and shuddered with her spasms, he was kneeing her thighs farther apart and guiding himself into her with frantic haste. His buttocks tensed and flexed at the first touch of her dewy wetness and then he drove into her, measuring his full length once, twice, and then again. She was as tight as a true virgin, and she felt so damn good clasping him within her pulsing body, so hot and wet . . . he had wanted this to last, but he was too far gone to wait. He could feel tiny fingers of fulfillment dancing up his spine, and then he was groaning out his own completion as his hard body slammed into her again and again, releasing his pent-up needs in jetting succession.

Annie lay quiescent beneath his greater weight for long moments in the dim room as his harsh, gasping breaths gradually resumed a more normal respiratory pattern. Her arms and legs were still wrapped tightly around him and she savored the intimacy of lying like this, still holding him within her. Tears trailed from the corners of her eyes as she relived the beauty of their lovemaking in her mind. Dane's head lay heavily on her breasts; she tenderly passed one hand through the wavy tumult of black silk locks.

As her movement registered on his sated senses, he lazily lifted his head, propping himself on his elbows above her without separating himself from her body. An inky eyebrow quirked in concern as he saw the tracks of tears slowly disappearing into the moist russet curls at her temples.

Dane groaned. "Did I hurt you?" He had thought she was aroused enough to accommodate him comfortably; he would never forgive himself if he had so crucially misjudged her physical readiness. He heaved his big body up onto his forearms, preparing to disengage himself, but she only tightened her limbs around him, the deceptively fragile-looking legs exerting pressure to keep him deeply inside her.

She linked her arms behind his head and pulled him down for a slow, sweet kiss that reassured him before she even opened her mouth to speak and he relaxed his tensed muscles again. "No, you didn't hurt me, you silly man." She smiled up at him through the tears. "I just didn't know...I've never...it was never that good for me." She settled on the evasive terminology with a small shrug.

Awareness flared in Dane's intense blue gaze. He understood what she hadn't explicitly stated. It explained the curious air of innocence he had sensed in her repeatedly, despite the fact that he knew she'd been married. "That makes me very happy," he said gently.

It was true. Knowing that she had reached ultimate satisfaction for the first time in his arms made him feel manly and proud and possessive in a manner he'd never felt before. It also made him feel like doing the same thing again, he reflected in amazement. He glanced down to see her blue eyes round in surprise, then he could almost read the anticipatory expression on her face as she wriggled experimentally underneath him. He chuckled, feeling a heady pleasure in his unexpected ability to renew their lovemaking. The chuckle died abruptly as another surge of arousal swept through him, tightening his body in a rush of desire. He bent his dark head to her breast and her fingers rose to clench convulsively in the thick strands of his hair. Together they moved again in a silent dance of love punctuated only by the creak of the bedsprings and the slide of body on body.

She woke from a dreamless sleep in the middle of the night. For an instant, she was confused by the hard weight pinning her middle. Then, as she grasped an arm and felt crisp curling hair overlying warm skin and sinew, memory came flooding back.

Dane. They'd made love. She felt . . . she felt guilty, as thoughts of Nick replaced the contented languor with which she had awoken.

But why should she allow herself to be ruled by guilt for the rest of her life? Nick wasn't here. She had loved him, had never wished him gone. But he was.

And now she had Dane. He'd overwhelmed her at first. If she was honest, he still did. But she was drawn to him in a way she'd never experienced before, not

The TV is by Panasonic, and loaded with features! It has a high contrast 13" picture tube, comes with a remote control with on–screen displays. This TV even has a sleep timer! All in all, it's terrific! We'll be giving away 50 free TVs to prompt respondents. And we'll send _you_ one, just for being picked as one of the fastest to reply!

Affix sticker to front of reply card and mail promptly!

PANASONIC COLOR TV WITH REMOTE

◄ Claim your free books, free gift and try for a free Color TV today! Return this card promptly! ►

# FREE TVs GIVEAWAY!

**H**ere's a chance to get a free Color TV! And here's a chance to get **four free Silhouette Desire® novels** from the Silhouette Reader Service™!

We'll send you four free books so you can see that we're like **no ordinary book club!** With the Reader Service, you never have to buy anything. You could even accept the free books and cancel immediately. In that case you'll owe nothing and be under no obligation!

Thousands of readers **enjoy** receiving books by mail. They like the home delivery ... they like getting the novels **months before** they're available in bookstores ... and they love our **discount prices!**

Try us and see! Peel off the label from the TV above and stick it on the front of this reply card in the space provided. Be sure to fill in your name and address below and RETURN YOUR CARD PROMPTLY! We'll send you your free books and a free gift, under the terms explained on the back. And we'll also enter you in the drawing for the Free Color TV's (SEE BACK OF BOOK FOR FREE TV DETAILS). We hope that you'll want to remain a subscriber—but the choice is always yours.

225 CIS AQ4Z
(TVL-S-10/94)

Name _____

Address _____

City _____ State _____ Zip Code _____

☐ NO. Do not send me four books and a gift. Enter me into the Fast TV draw.

Book offer not valid to current Silhouette Desire subscribers. All orders subject to approval.

Printed in the USA

© 1994 Harlequin Enterprises Ltd.

**AFFIX TV STICKER HERE**

Office use only

:

/

POSTAGE WILL BE PAID BY ADDRESSEE

**BUSINESS REPLY MAIL**
FIRST CLASS MAIL    PERMIT NO. 717    BUFFALO, NY

SILHOUETTE READER SERVICE
FAST TV SWEEPSTAKES OFFER
P.O. BOX 9010
BUFFALO, NY 14240-9935

NO POSTAGE
NECESSARY
IF MAILED
IN THE
UNITED STATES

even with Nick. Her mind shied away from labeling what she felt for him—it was too soon for grand pronouncements. But she knew that her life had been altered completely and unchangeably by what had passed between them tonight. She was his now, if he wanted her.

She found herself avoiding any thought of how she'd feel if he didn't.

The warm weight of him against her distracted her from deeper thought. He had merely shifted his considerable weight to one side and pulled her into the curve of his naked frame to sleep after the second time they made love. He still had one leg thrown across her. Her head was pillowed on a bulging bicep and the other large hand cupped a breast possessively. She smiled quietly.

Then her thoughts turned to more mundane concerns. Mother Nature's call could no longer be ignored and she carefully slid from his arms to the side of the bed. He stretched and rolled over onto his stomach, burying his head under a pillow. Shaking her head in amusement, she walked silently across the floor to the bathroom.

Returning to the bed a moment later, she began to slide back in as stealthily as she had gotten out. When a large hand yanked her suddenly over to sprawl across his chest, she gave a startled squeak.

"I thought you were still sleeping," she said breathlessly.

"I couldn't sleep without you in my arms." He rubbed his chin against the top of her head.

She kissed his collarbone, wondering what to say, opting for a light reply. "Guess you'll have to keep me around so you can get your beauty rest."

"You bet, baby. Now that I've finally got you, I'm not planning to let you go. You're stuck with me for good."

A warm glow spread through her. He did want to be with her! What did he mean by, "for good?" She couldn't think of anything to say that wouldn't reveal how much his words meant to her, so she said nothing, choosing instead to lay her head on his shoulder.

A pregnant silence followed his words. Hell, he thought. He hadn't meant to rush her; those words had just slipped out. He guessed it was a good sign that she hadn't pulled away, but had instead settled herself against him like a small cat. But what was she thinking? Cautiously, he asked, "No response?"

She lifted her head from where she'd been cuddled against him and made eye contact for the first time. He could just barely see her eyes, wide and serious, in the darkness. "Define 'for good.'"

He measured her face. "As in 'til death do us part."

Another silence descended and he could feel the fine tension that had invaded her limbs. Then, when he was about to turn on the light so that he could gauge her expression to see how badly he had handled this, she responded once more. "You've obviously forgotten a few crucial details. Why don't I explain how a marriage proposal should be tendered?"

Letting out a deep breath he hadn't realized he was holding, he laughed and rolled her beneath him, settling himself familiarly between her legs. "I think I can take it from here. Do you mind if I forego the part where I get down on one knee?" To emphasize his words, he lifted his hips slightly. The blunt flesh of his newly revived arousal probed at the hidden entrance to her and she willingly lifted her bottom to receive the evidence of his need for her. They both gasped as he slid slowly, deliciously into her, not stopping until he was fully sheathed in her moist depths.

"I haven't been able to get you out of my mind for weeks," he growled against her lips. "I know this is sudden, but I know what I want, and I want you to marry me."

He still hadn't actually *asked*, she noted, and he hadn't said he loved her.

Apparently he read her hesitation as refusal, because he said, "Think before you decide. We'd be perfect for each other. You want children, so do I. You love this house, so do I. If you marry me, you can have both those things. I don't mind your career. We turn each other on so totally, no one else is ever going to be able to compare."

"I know." Her voice was a thin thread. "But what about . . . love?"

For the first time, she felt his big shoulders stiffen where she'd laid her hands against them. "Love doesn't exist," he said, and his tone was harsher than any she'd ever heard him use. "We're compatible in all the ways that count. Isn't that a lot more important than an emotion that could change tomorrow?"

In the darkness, he could feel her withdrawing from him mentally, though his flesh still claimed hers. "I don't know," she whispered.

A surge of panic crashed over his head. She couldn't refuse him—he needed her. Nobody else would do. Dropping his head, he sought her mouth with single-minded determination. "Let me convince you," he whispered against her lips.

Morning light was streaming into the bedroom when Dane opened his eyes again. He gave a cursory glance around the quietly tasteful room before turning his attention to the woman still sleeping in his arms.

Nothing would bring him more pleasure than to come home to her at the end of every day. He had to restrain himself from clutching her in a fiercely pos-sessive hug as the memory of their lovemaking rever-berated in his head.

She slept deeply as he watched her, deriving im-mense pleasure from simply holding her. That glori-ous hair was spread wildly out across the pillow, trailing over her shoulders and fanning across his own chest in fiery disarray. The sweet bow of her mobile lips was slightly parted and he could see the serrated edges of pearly teeth that he recalled had nipped in abandon at his neck last night. The sheets were tan-gled low at their hips and her upper torso was bared to his gaze. She had the creamiest skin he had ever en-countered. He could trace the delicate network of veins beneath the fine-grained flesh and his eyes fol-lowed those life-giving vessels to the crest of one breast. Her nipples were a deep shade of rose-pink, capping the ripe mounds like cherries on an ice-cream sundae. Idly his thoughts wandered to the future and he imagined how those beautiful breasts would look full of milk for an infant. A baby...made by the same act of intimacy they had shared last night. He pictured a strapping son with his mother's blue eyes and hair of flame.

The smile froze on his face as he suddenly realized what his driving desire to possess her had led him to forget last night. Hell! Raising his head slightly, his eyes confirmed what his brain had just remembered. The incriminating foil packet lay undisturbed on the nightstand right where he had dropped it beside his wallet. He had had the presence of mind to put protection within easy reach but he had been so caught up in the responsive movements of the perfect little figure nestled next to him that all thought of birth control had gone right out of his head.

A telling statement, he reflected without amusement. He had always been scrupulously careful about such things for his own protection as well as his partner's. The very fact that he could forget necessary measures like that showed him how very deeply this woman had gotten under his skin.

Beside him, Annie stirred, perhaps sensing his disquiet. Blue eyes snapped open as her body protested movement and she recalled the events of last night. A red tide of color swept up her neck and tinged her cheeks as she forced herself to meet his gaze. "Good morning."

"Good morning," he returned, squeezing her gently. "I can't believe you can still blush like that after the things we did last night. Do you remember when you—''

"Dane!"

He laughed and she smiled tentatively. That smile relaxed nerves he hadn't even realized were strung tight. She didn't look like a woman who was going to turn down his proposal. And if she was a little less delighted about it than he'd hoped, he figured she'd been taken by surprise. Well, that would soon pass.

"If I tell you how beautiful you look with your hair all mussed, will you kiss me?"

In answer, she turned in his embrace to press her lips as high along his jaw as she could reach. Shifting her to her back, he leaned over her and leisurely explored her mouth in a potent kiss that had her breath coming faster when he finally lifted his head.

"Much as I would love to keep you in bed all day, I know it's not practical," he informed her. "Especially if you want to be able to walk tomorrow!"

Annie smiled shyly. "I have to be able to walk," she reminded him. "I have classes tomorrow."

"And we have plans to make."

"Dane . . ." Her eyes shifted away from his.

"Annie. . ." He took her chin in one hand and raised her face to his. "I want you more than any woman I've ever met. I want a life with you. Marry me."

"I can't make that decision right now," she said, and he was surprised by the strength of her objection. It shook him more than he wanted to admit. "I have to have time to think about this." She smiled at him. "If I let you railroad me into this, you'll think you can get away with it for the rest of our lives."

It wasn't what he wanted to hear, but her final sentence gave him hope. He decided to give her one last gentle nudge. "I won't promise not to try to influence your decision, but I'll respect your need to think it through. I know what I'm asking is a big step for both of us. But don't make me wait too long—we may have a need for haste."

When she raised uncomprehending eyes to his again, he smiled wryly and gestured sheepishly to the bedside table. As she turned her head to see what he meant, he went on. "You got me in such a dither last night that I completely forgot to take any precautions. Although we hadn't discussed starting a family right away, it doesn't bother me in the least." His hand slid tenderly down to rest just above where he knew their child could already be forming. "As a matter of fact, I can't think of anything that would make me happier than to see your body carrying my child."

She was silent again and he could almost see her counting in her head, though he couldn't tell how she felt about his words. Finally, she said, "No, it's the wrong time."

"That's just as well. I'd like to be married before we start a family."

"Dane..." Her voice trailed away helplessly. "I might not be able to have children as easily as you imagine." Reaching for his hand, she placed it over her abdomen. "Feel that?"

He did. For the first time, he noticed the distinctive ridge of scar tissue beneath his fingers. Pulling back, he looked down at the long, ugly scar that marred her smooth skin.

"It's from the accident," she said. "Everything was repaired to the surgeon's satisfaction, but afterward I contracted some kind of infection that invaded one of my fallopian tubes. I've been told that although I can still bear children, my chances of conception are about fifty percent now."

He only half understood what she was saying. His mind was reeling. He hadn't realized that she'd been injured in the accident that had claimed her husband's and dog's lives, hadn't realized that she must have been a hairbreadth from death herself.

"My God," he said, and his voice was hoarse with shock. "You could have died, too."

Annie nodded. "But—"

"Hey! Sweet sister of mine! Could I con you into making me an early breakfast this morning?"

"What the hell is he doing here?" Dane growled, reaching for his pants.

Annie scrambled out of bed and he caught a flash of sleek, pale skin before she struggled into a flannel robe. "I'll get rid of him," she said.

Dane finished dressing slowly, listening to Annie's footsteps receding down the steps. The shock of what she'd just told him was still reverberating in his head. For the first time, he acknowledged to himself that he didn't want to live without Annie for the rest of his life. Somehow, she'd become more important to him than any woman since Amanda—hell, she was more important than that! He'd wanted Amanda physically, fiercely in the early days of their marriage. But he couldn't remember ever *caring* about her the way he cared about Annie. Knowing that she'd nearly died was a horrifying thought.

The sound of voices downstairs prompted him to open the door and start down the hall. He realized Patrick probably hadn't seen his car, parked behind the house as it was. He wasn't entirely sure he liked the way Annie had leaped to head off her brother. To him, the sooner they told people, the better. It would give him one more way to bind Annie to him.

# Six

"Sorry, I'm not going to have time for breakfast this morning," Annie told her brother firmly.

Patrick was already busy pouring water into the coffeemaker he'd just filled. "Aw, come on," he said. "It's only seven-thirty. What have you got to do so early?" He turned and gave her an angelic smile. "I was afraid you couldn't make breakfast without me."

Annie snorted. "Fat chance. More likely you didn't have any food of your own so you decided to come mooch from me." But she smiled at him. Breakfast together had been a part of their routine when they'd shared the house. This was Patrick's way of checking up on her, making sure she was doing all right on her own, and she couldn't be mad at him for caring.

But she really had to get rid of him!

Patrick was opening the refrigerator. "How about if I make some scrambled eggs since you're in such a hurry? You can run and get dressed and we can eat together."

"Patrick, I really don't have time." Annie crossed to him and put a hand on his elbow. "How about tomorrow? You can come over, and I'll make you the biggest breakfast you've ever had."

"You might as well let him stay. I'll make western omelets. Bet you didn't know I'm a mean hand with a skillet."

The deep voice froze Patrick in his turn from the refrigerator. He clutched the carton of eggs he was holding with both hands.

Annie's hand fell away from her brother's arm. She'd been so worried about getting Patrick to leave that she hadn't heard Dane come into the kitchen behind her.

Slowly, Patrick set down the eggs and turned to face Dane. Annie did the same, taking in Dane's proprietary air and the fact that he was acting as if his presence in her house this early in the morning were an ordinary occurrence.

He was lounging against the doorframe with one foot crossed over the other, looking supremely relaxed. But she read the silent challenge in the blue eyes he leveled on her brother.

Patrick cleared his throat. "Good morning, Hamilton. Fancy meeting you here."

Annie closed her eyes. Dear heaven. Her normally easygoing brother had a protective streak a mile wide and she could tell from his flat, almost deadly tone of voice that he was bent on protecting her now. Patrick might deceive other people with the laid-back, humorous front he presented to the world, but she knew that beneath the surface was an unwavering implacability that sprang into action whenever he perceived a threat to someone he loved. And right now, that someone was her.

''I could say the same. Don't you have a home of your own?'' Dane's tone was equally cool.

She opened her eyes again to see him smile, but it wasn't a warm, friendly expression. No, it was more a baring of the teeth. And Patrick reacted accordingly. She was used to reading signs of aggression in dogs and these two weren't acting much differently—she could almost see each man bristling his fur and trying to outstare the other.

''I may have a home of my own, but I still consider my sister my responsibility,'' Patrick said. He took a step forward and Annie hastily grabbed his arm. ''I won't let her be taken advantage of.''

''Your sister is an adult. She can make her own decisions.'' It was almost as if Dane were deliberately goading Patrick into a fight.

''Stop it, Dane.'' Her tone was sharp and irritated. From the back porch, Ebony barked sharply, responding to the sound of distress in her mistress's voice. ''And you stop it, too, Patrick.'' Again she tried to take Patrick's arm and pull him away, but her brother's feet were planted in an aggressive stance and her tug on his arm had less effect than a gnat landing on it.

The room was silent except for the breathing of the two men. Then Dane turned away and pulled out a stool at the breakfast bar, taking one opposite for himself. "Have a seat, Murphy. We need to talk."

"I'll say we do," Patrick growled. He went toward the stool, but Annie could tell he was still on the offensive. She held her breath, wondering what Dane would do next.

When he looked across at her and held out a hand, she stood for a moment, confused. But the silent command focused on her overrode her objections and she crossed to him, allowing him to take her hand in his and pull her to his side.

"I've asked your sister to be my wife." Dane switched his gaze back to Patrick, and a note of humor replaced the tone he'd used earlier. "Granted, it means I'll be related to you, but I thought it over and decided she was worth it."

If she'd been in the mood to laugh, the classic look of shock on Patrick's face would have been just what she needed. His mouth actually dropped open and his blue eyes widened. After a moment, he looked at her.

"Is that true?" he demanded. "Are you going to marry him?"

"Well," she hedged, "I haven't agreed yet, but the topic is under discussion." To Dane, she said, "If you think just because you've announced this to my brother that you can rush my decision, you can think again. I told you I wouldn't be hurried into anything."

When she glanced back at Patrick, for the first time his face held a hint of its usual lightness. "Isn't this kind of quick?" he asked.

"Yes," she said.

"No," said Dane simultaneously. "Not quick enough by a long shot."

Patrick looked from one to the other of them, and his gaze was dancing with humor. "You're going to have your hands full," he said to Dane.

"I know."

Annie huffed out a breath of disgust and pulled herself away from his side. "You two are ridiculous. Two minutes ago, you were ready to tear into each other, now you're the best of buddies again."

"I can't fight with my future brother-in-law," Patrick said reasonably.

"What happened to the Great Protector?"

"You don't need to be protected from the man if you're going to marry him."

"We haven't made any decisions," she said through her teeth.

Patrick didn't even hear her. "I knew you were perfect for each other."

"You did not." Annie flicked the end of a dish towel at him.

"Oh, yes, I did. Why do you think I invited him to that barbecue?" He dodged the dish towel when she flung it at him and held up three fingers. "If we're having omelets, I'd like a three-egg platter."

As if in agreement, they all dropped the subject of marriage after that and conversation was general over the meal. As soon as breakfast ended, Patrick excused himself and headed for work.

"Thanks for letting me intrude on you two lovebirds," he said cheerily as he banged out the back door.

Annie shifted uneasily, wondering if Dane intended to announce that there was no love involved in his decision to marry her. But he acted as if he hadn't absorbed what Patrick said.

Instead, he looked at his watch. "I have to go home and shower and change," he grumbled. "I'd rather stay here with you all day. Can we have dinner tonight?"

Annie nodded. "I don't have classes on Monday nights." She gasped as he pulled her into his arms. "But the rest of the week will be kind of hectic," she added. He lifted her until she fit snugly against him and she closed her eyes, her thoughts scattering.

He nuzzled her neck. "I'll bring clothes with me tonight. And my dog. Then I won't have to rush off and leave you tomorrow morning." He dropped his head and kissed her possessively. "Is that okay with you?"

Annie nodded, too dazed to protest. At his request, she even gave him a key in case she was still at the training center when he arrived after work. When the front door closed behind him, she walked slowly back to feed Ebony and clean up the kitchen.

What was she going to do? Dane was aggravating, exciting, compelling. She couldn't resist him. In her heart, she knew she'd said a fond goodbye to her

memories of Nick the first time Dane kissed her...
because she was falling in love with him.

She should be happy. She should be ecstatic! He
wanted to marry her. He desired her.

But he didn't love her, didn't believe in love. He'd
been clear about that. And worse yet, he didn't want
her love. On the other hand, he was offering her a
second chance at children of her own. She had no
doubt he'd be a devoted family man. But could she
live without love?

She had three private lessons scheduled that afternoon and the first one ran late. That backed up the
other two and she got home later than she'd planned.
She was dirty and she smelled like dog, so she opted
for a quick shower before Dane arrived.

She was toweling herself dry when the phone rang.
Heading into the bedroom, she flopped across the bed
to reach the receiver.

It was a potential client calling for information and
she had to dig in the drawer of the bedside table for a
pencil and pad to take down the lady's address.

"I'll be happy to send you our brochure," she told
the woman. "It has a list of classes and times in it and
you can come observe a few times before you make
any decisions about enrolling your dog." She was just
hanging up the receiver when the bedroom door swung
open behind her.

Annie jumped. Twisting her head around, she saw
Dane framed in the doorway. She felt horribly self-
conscious, wrapped only in the bath towel she'd
thrown around herself when the telephone rang, but

at the same time she was aware of her near nakedness in a deeply feminine way.

When her gaze met Dane's she saw that he was equally aware of what she wasn't wearing. A thrill of excitement flashed through her, tightening her nipples into hard pebbles. His face flushed and his nostrils flared slightly, as if scenting her arousal. She felt a heavy, throbbing sensation deep in her abdomen and she simply lay waiting, unable to make herself move as he strode to the edge of the bed in three long strides.

He'd looked in the kitchen and all through the downstairs before coming up to the bedroom. When he had opened the door, he had been stunned to find Annie lying on her stomach across the bed with only a small towel for cover. He could see the rounded swell of her satiny bottom and the enticing shadows of feminine folds between her legs. Instantly, he was so hard he ached and when she squirmed slightly, he knew he had to have her. Approaching the bed, he held her blue gaze as he deliberately unzipped his pants and popped the snap at the waistband.

The small sounds echoed in the silence of the sunny room. Her eyes rounded even more as he pushed his pants and his briefs down in one motion and reached for her. She drew in a sobbing breath as his hands closed around her ankles and then he was pulling her back over the bed, separating her legs on either side of his lean hips until the pulsing life of his manhood was eagerly nudging the soft curling hair inside her thighs. He bent over her, pulling the towel away and dropping it on the floor, sliding both hands under her to gently rub and squeeze her nipples and palming the generous weight of her breasts in satisfaction.

Annie cried out and her back arched as she clenched fistfuls of the quilt. He slid one big hand down her stomach, burrowing underneath her shifting hips to circle the tiny bud of flesh he found with a sure, intimate touch that had her gasping. She bucked wildly beneath him and he groaned, unable to control his body a minute longer as the clasp of her flexing buttocks held and released him rhythmically.

Frantically, he tore open the small packet still lying untouched on the nightstand and donned its contents. He had intended to turn her over, to suck at those pretty breasts and kiss the full lip that he could see caught between her teeth as she turned her head from side to side, but instead he grasped her thighs, pressing his aroused length into the slick moisture of her depths, inexorably filling her as she continued to rub her soft bottom against the black hair that bloomed at the juncture of his legs. He withdrew frantically and began a driving rhythm that quickly brought him to the edge, but he wanted her to be with him, so again he found the tight button below the triangle of copper curls and stimulated her.

She was so wildly sensitive that at the first touch of his finger the storm broke and her body jerked in ecstasy. Feeling the inner clenching that signaled her release was all he needed and his own body followed her to a pulsing fulfillment that drove him more deeply into her with each forceful spasm.

Gradually the world stopped spinning and Annie became aware of her surroundings again. Her cheek was pressed into the quilt that covered the bed. Dane had collapsed on her and he groaned as she purposely tightened her inner muscles in an unseen caress.

"Don't you ever know when to quit?" he teased. Gently withdrawing from her, he found his feet just long enough to flop onto the bed beside her and pull her across his chest. Her long hair clung to the sweat-dampened muscles of his stomach as she angled her head to look up at him.

"Apparently not," she answered his joking query. Then she looked at him again, shaking her head and smiling, though her cheeks were pink. "Do you realize you're still wearing a tie?"

He laughed. "A few minutes ago, I had more important things on my mind than my attire." Then he rolled to a sitting position, effortlessly righting her to sit beside him on the edge of the rumpled bed and she could almost feel the restless energy radiating from him. "Let's get dressed and go hunting for engagement rings. I'd like to have one on your finger as soon as possible. We could look at wedding rings, as well. I've decided I'd like to wear one, too."

Annie glanced at him from beneath her lashes. He sounded as confident and self-assured as usual, but he was watching her with a surprisingly vulnerable look in his blue eyes...almost as if he was afraid she would say no.

She took a deep breath. There was no point in making him wait for her answer. She might have reservations about the wisdom of marriage to Dane, but she loved him . . . so much that she'd take him with no love if that was the only way she could have him.

"All right," she said. "I'll marry you. Let's go look for rings."

The following fortnight was a whirlwind of activity. Once he'd talked her into marrying him, Dane seemed determined to mesh their lives as quickly as possible. Each evening when Annie returned from her night classes, he'd moved a few more of his possessions into the house they'd decided to keep. His dog's crate was installed next to Ebony's and Dane and Annie spent several evenings catching the late news with the two black dogs stretched out on the floor at their feet. And when the news ended, he carried her to their bed and made passionate love to her every single night, worshiping her body with a single-minded intensity that reassured her that this decision was right for them both.

He produced a marriage license and set up a time for the civil ceremony they'd agreed on at Oak Park Courthouse. Joe, Jeanne and Patrick would be their only witnesses and it was Dane's suggestion to postpone honeymoon plans until the Christmas holidays so that Annie's classes wouldn't be disrupted.

On the day of the wedding, they dressed together in the big bedroom they were sharing now.

Dane fumbled with the hook and eye at the back of her pale yellow silk suit for several seconds before he finally succeeded in maneuvering the tiny catch into place. "There." He dropped a kiss onto the back of her neck beneath the coil into which she'd pinned her hair. "Are you ready to go?"

Annie turned to face him, loving the way he'd brushed his dark curls down and the serious blue eyes he turned on her.

"I'm ready." She picked up her matching purse, then something else caught her eye, a final detail she'd overlooked in the mad rush of the past few weeks. Walking back to her dresser, she picked up the picture of Nick that stood there in a small silver frame.

Gently, she touched the smiling features, so hard to recall with clarity anymore. She'd loved him with all her heart, would always carry the memories with her, but now her heart belonged to Dane. Silently, she said goodbye as she opened a drawer and placed the frame facedown inside. Dane was watching her as she turned to him once more. "I'm ready," she said again.

He nodded, coming across the room to place both hands lightly on her shoulders. "You won't regret this marriage," he said in a deep tone. "I promise you that I'll take care of you and our family."

And he would, she was sure. He'd be a wonderful husband and father. And if he couldn't love her as she'd once been loved, at least she'd have the pleasure of giving him children they could share. As surely as she knew her love for him would never die, she knew he would love their children with every fiber of his soul.

On a Saturday one week after their wedding, Dane met her at the training center at noon. She had a class at ten and another at eleven on Saturday, but they'd arranged to go into Chicago after her second class ended.

He walked into the big room where she held classes just as the last few students were leaving.

"See you next week, Mrs. Hamilton," called one of the students. A primitive surge of satisfaction ran through him at the name—he still had trouble believing she was really his except when she lay beside him in the big bed at night. They were going to Peoria tomorrow to have dinner with some of his best friends. They'd been a little miffed that he hadn't told them he was getting married until after the fact, but he'd been afraid, in some part of his mind that he barely dared to acknowledge, that she might change her mind at the last minute. A woman had made a fool of him once—never again.

"I'm almost ready." Annie gave him an intimate smile that warmed him and turned him on at the same time. He'd forgotten how satisfying being married could be. Or perhaps he'd never really known it before, with Amanda. He couldn't recall ever feeling the inner glow that Annie's smile produced, the sense of well-being that merely holding her in the night or kissing her at the door gave him. He could barely remember Amanda anymore, but he knew that most of what had driven their relationship had been based, purely and simply, on sex. And when that had worn off, they hadn't had much in common. They hadn't even really liked each other all that well, if he were honest.

He couldn't imagine ever tiring of Annie in any way.

Of course, tiring of her would entail seeing a lot more of her than he currently did, he thought, only half-amused. In the month since he'd moved in with her, into the house they referred to now as "theirs," he'd realized just how much of Annie's time was consumed by her business.

A lot. She taught classes Tuesday through Friday evenings as well as several more during those days, and these two on Saturday morning. Although Sunday and Monday were technically her days off, he knew she often set up private lessons on Monday. It was a bad combination with his typical day, which ran from early morning until four-thirty in the afternoon with occasional evening meetings.

Oh, well. He'd known what he was getting into when he'd married her. Children would complicate things, but when kids came along, they'd find a good nanny and work out the details when the need arose.

Annie came out of the office then with her jacket and a purse. She usually wore jeans to teach, but today she'd dressed up a little since he'd offered to take her out to lunch. She looked pretty, if a little tired, in her pink sweater and gray slacks.

They drove down to South Chicago first, to a renovated warehouse that sold salvaged grillwork and decorative embellishments. Wandering through the place was fascinating. There were literally thousands of pieces of grillwork, none matching and only a few large enough to fence a very small yard. Annie finally chose a piece with cherubs welded into the grill to have fashioned into a gate to hang between the stone pillars that led to the enclosed backyard. On the way out, a stone urn caught his eye and Annie was easily convinced that it would look wonderful on the front steps.

As they headed for the car, staggering under the weight of their purchases, someone hailed him.

"Hey, Dane! Doing a little shopping?"

Dane recognized William Machlowski, the head of computer operations at the bank. He headed toward them, towing his wife...Cheryl or something like that. He vaguely remembered meeting her at a cocktail party weeks ago.

William bustled over and Dane set down the urn and the grillwork in time to have his hand pumped enthusiastically. "See you made some purchases. We're down here to look at a griffin Sherry insists we have to have. You do remember my wife?" He indicated the blonde at his side.

Dane nodded politely. "Nice to see you again. I believe you've met my wife, Annie."

Annie smiled. "Hello."

"Hel-*lo!* And congratulations on snaring this hunk! Charlene was absolutely livid when she heard." The blonde giggled.

"Actually," Dane said, "it was the other way around. I had to beg her to marry me."

"Oh, you." Sherry slapped his forearm playfully. "Isn't he silly, Will?" Then she looked back at Annie again. "This is just perfect timing. I was going to call you this week. We have an opening in our weekly girls' bridge club and we decided you'd be the perfect one to fill it."

There was an awkward pause, then Annie said, "I'm so sorry, but I don't play bridge."

"You don't play...*everyone* plays bridge. Well, no matter, I suppose we can teach you." Sherry sounded truly perplexed by such a problem. "Where *have* you been living, dear?"

He wanted to laugh aloud at the expression on Annie's face. She clearly couldn't figure out how to extricate herself from the woman's insistence. He couldn't imagine being condemned to play bridge with Sherry and her friends every week.

"She doesn't have the time for card games." Dane wrapped his free arm around Annie. "My wife owns a business that takes up most of her days, and I'm afraid I want all of her free time to be devoted to me."

William laughed too heartily. "Sounds good to me."

Dane felt a little sorry for the man. He couldn't see Sherry Machlowski devoting time to anyone other than herself.

"Well, if you're sure..." William's wife clearly thought Annie was missing a great opportunity.

"Dane's right. I am too busy. But it was thoughtful of you to think of me."

Annie's voice rang with sincerity but he knew relief was just beneath the surface.

"We have to be going," Dane said. "Good seeing you both."

"You, too," Sherry echoed. As her husband led her away, she said to Annie, "Just be sure you don't let your business interfere with your wifely duties, dear."

As soon as the other couple were out of earshot, he turned to Annie with a big grin. "Let's have lunch. Then we'll go home and you can brush up on your 'wifely duties.'"

* * *

They drove down to the Art Institute for lunch in the enclosed garden room. The weather was tricky at this time of year, but the day was warm for autumn and the restaurant was open. The classical notes of a piano sonata floated across the air as they were seated.

Beautiful fall flowers had been planted in the tubs and beds near the tables, but Annie barely noticed her surroundings. She ordered absently and sat silently as Dane did the same.

She thought he was enjoying the atmosphere and the music, when he abruptly reached across the table and clasped her hand.

"What's wrong?"

Startled, she looked up. He was looking at her expectantly and she knew if she tried to dodge the issue, he'd worry her until she gave in, anyway.

She sighed. "Seeing Sherry again got me thinking about things I've managed to ignore since we got married. But I can't forget them forever. Sooner or later, you're going to be sorry you married me."

Dane looked dumbfounded and uncomprehending. "What do you think you've done that's going to make me change the way I feel about our marriage?"

"It's not what I've done. . . ." She sighed again. He really didn't get it. "It's more like what I don't do."

"What you don't do?"

"Yes." She leaned forward. "That conversation earlier reminded me of how inept I am socially. I was never good at the stuff lawyers' wives are supposed to do and now I'm married to a banker and I'm even worse!"

Dane looked perplexed. When she would have pulled her hand away, he held on with a grip she couldn't break. "What kind of stuff are lawyers' and bankers' wives supposed to do?"

"You know." How could he be so obtuse? "Entertaining. Chitchat." Misery swamped her. "I'm terrible at talking to people I don't know. I don't want to embarrass you. And what if your bosses are looking for a man with a wife who can handle all those social functions when they're trying to decide who to promote?"

Dane was looking at her as if she'd just flown in from another planet. He let her hand slide from his this time when she tugged. "Let me get this straight. You're afraid that you could hurt my chances for advancement if you don't play the games that the other wives do?"

That was it in a nutshell, though he'd missed a few points. She nodded.

"Annie..." Dane lifted his shoulders in a gesture of total male frustration. "That's the craziest thing I have ever heard. I don't think you have to worry about affecting my job. Besides, you socialized just fine with Lilith at the cocktail party, if I recall correctly."

"Only because she liked to talk about dogs."

"So what? You talked to her, didn't you?" Then his blue eyes sharpened. "You think I want you to play cards with William's wife and her friends?" He waved a hand dismissively. "Forget it. You might come home with that manic giggle."

Annie almost laughed but she was still too upset. "I'm afraid I might embarrass you," she mumbled.

"Sweetheart—" Dane reached across the table again and took both of her hands "—you'll never embarrass me. Every man we meet is too busy noticing how beautiful you are, and the wives are too busy noticing their husbands noticing to be thinking about what you are or aren't saying."

"I'm not beautiful," she said automatically.

"You are to me," he responded. "Now quit worrying about something so trivial. I don't care if you hate to socialize. I'm not wild about it, either. We'll just make sure we do as little of it as possible."

Their meal arrived then and she let the conversation drop. His words had reassured her, but she still worried that she might be a burden to his career. Then another thought struck her, less palatable even than those that were worrying her.

Dane hadn't married her for her social prowess. He'd married her for her reproductive capabilities and for that alone. She knew he wanted children as soon as possible. Glancing across the table, she watched him tearing into the double-decker sandwich he'd ordered. Just then, he looked up, and catching her staring, he shot her a wink and a grin.

Her heart squeezed in pain. She loved him so much. When had he come to be her whole world? And was there any chance that he would ever come to love her?

On the way out of the Art Institute, they walked through a room displaying a medieval collection. Dane seemed to want to linger as they examined suits of mail, lances for jousting and horribly heavy-looking shields of decorated metal.

"This one might fit you," he told her as they marveled over one suit of armor.

"Men certainly were much smaller a century ago," she said.

"Funny the things you learn as an adult that destroy the romance," he responded.

"Such as?"

"Just what you said about men being smaller. When I was a kid, I was fascinated by the Arthurian legends. One of my foster mothers was always reading me stories about the Knights of the Round Table and their chivalrous deeds."

"Camelot."

"The perfect court for the perfect king."

Annie smiled at him. "I used to think of my marriage to Nick as Camelot. I haven't thought about that in a long time."

He shook his head, gazing absently at the armor. "You can't imagine how I envy you those memories."

"Well," she said, shrugging, ill at ease and sorry she'd brought up the topic of first marriages. "Nick and I never really fought. I don't know why."

"My ex-wife and I fought enough for two lifetimes."

She was painfully aware that he'd told her next to nothing about his past with the first woman he'd married. She'd been curious but the opportunity for such a discussion had never presented itself before. "What kind of things did you fight about?"

No answer.

She glanced at his face and was immediately chilled by the closed look he wore. Dane was usually so open and even-tempered—

"We fought about a lot of things." His tone was mild and his face, when she looked again, was composed into its normal expression. But something final in his tone warned her that this particular line of inquiry was finished.

She wondered what he'd suffered at the hands of his first wife that could make him look like that.

# Seven

Annie's schedule was unchanged during the next week, except that she was a little busier than usual. It was the first week to register students for the winter-session classes and she had dozens of applications to check, organize into the proper session and file.

In addition to that, she had a touch of the flu.

It wasn't a severe case, because she was able to function. But all week long, she suffered through nausea that at times made her feel she might have to dash for a bathroom. The funny thing was, she felt pretty good every morning. But by the time her classes began in the evening, she felt distinctly queasy, so much so that she couldn't eat dinner for three nights running. The other nights, she managed to get down some soup that she'd made over the weekend and re-heated when she was too busy to cook.

On Thursday, she had a Puppy Kindergarten class at four o'clock. Dane had gotten in the habit of bringing in sandwiches from the nearby deli about five-fifteen and they shared a meal and a few private moments before the Basic students from the class he was taking began to straggle in just before six.

This particular Thursday, Dane came breezing in as the last of the puppies was leaving.

"Hi." He greeted her with a quick kiss, which turned to concern when he got a look at her face. "You still aren't feeling well, are you?"

"No." She sank into her office chair. "Is it that obvious?"

"Other than the fact that your face is green, no."

She cast him a small smile. "Very funny. I hope I shake this soon. How was your day?"

Dane drew the sandwiches from the bag. "My day was interesting. We're considering a loan to a guy who owns a pretzel factory and I got a personal tour." He stuck two straws in the lemonade he'd brought and unwrapped the sandwiches. "Do you want pastrami or—Annie!"

The sight of the sandwich had done it. Her stomach, which hadn't been happy at all since about three o'clock, decided to rebel. Bolting out of her chair, she raced for the bathroom.

She barely made it. As she knelt on the floor in front of the toilet, Dane came in behind her. Silently he took a paper towel from the dispenser, wet it and handed it to her, then flushed the toilet.

"Thanks." She felt too ill to be embarrassed as she accepted the hand he extended to help her to her feet.

"Have you considered that you might be pregnant?"

She stared at him, openmouthed, calculating in her head. "I sincerely doubt it . . . oh!" She *had* missed a period, come to think of it, but she hadn't even thought about it in the turmoil of adjusting to married life. "I'm a little late," she admitted. "But it's way too early to tell."

"Not for a blood test it isn't."

Hope and excitement blossomed within her. "Yes," she said slowly. "I guess you're right."

She called the doctor's office first thing the next morning and the receptionist told her she could come in right away before she ate any breakfast.

As the woman at the doctor's office had instructed, Annie dutifully collected a urine sample. But right after Dane left for work, a disappointingly familiar sensation warned her that she was beginning her menstrual cycle. The light spotting she felt was only the beginning.

Her disappointment was intense as she changed her panties, more so than the occasion warranted. If she had been pregnant, it would have been from the one time before they were married—nearly five weeks ago now, wouldn't it? They had plenty of time to start a family.

If only Dane wasn't waiting to hear some news . . . she almost canceled the doctor's appointment, but she decided to go, anyway. Just to be sure.

The receptionist slid back the glass panel above the counter with a cheerful smile when Annie approached the desk in the obstetrician's office. "Hello. May I help you?"

Annie held up her little glass jar with a sheepish smile. "My name is Anne Elizabeth Hamilton. I'm here for a pregnancy test."

The receptionist took the jar and in a few moments, Annie was given a blood test. She explained to the nurse who was attending her that she had started her period, but when the nurse heard how late she was, she said, "Well, it can't hurt to be sure."

Annie fidgeted nervously when the woman left the room. On the wall was a chart showing a cross section of a pregnant woman with a fetus curled in her womb. Amazing. Another chart detailed how the tiny life grew, at what week a given body part budded on the tiny torso, when the baby's eyes opened and when it began to swallow. Yet a third chart listed types of birth control—not something she foresaw needing in the near future, she thought with a warm glow. It was nice not to have to worry about—

The door opened. The nurse had a slight smile on her face.

"Congratulations, Mrs. Hamilton. Your body might not have figured it out quite yet, but you are definitely pregnant."

"I am? That's wonderful!" Annie closed her eyes, feeling a thrill rush through her. Then her eyes popped open again. "But what about the bleeding?"

"Some women have a little spotting early on," the nurse told her as she set up a prenatal conference for the following month. "It's nothing to worry about unless it persists or you have a heavy flow. If that happens, call us right away. Otherwise—'' she patted Annie's hand and smiled ''—we'll see you in about a month.''

At nine-twenty she was walking out of the doctor's office in a daze, clutching a fistful of booklets and handouts on prenatal care.

Dane was in his office dictating a letter when he saw Annie coming down the hall. She had only been to the bank one time since they'd married. This time, the smile on her pretty face told him everything he needed to know.

Completely forgetting the secretary, he leaped to his feet and met her in the hall, sweeping her into his arms.

''Good news?''

''Good news,'' she confirmed.

He threw back his head and laughed aloud, spinning her around. ''I can't believe it! I'm going to be a father! We're going to be parents!''

Several of his co-workers had stuck their heads out of their office doors in response to the commotion; over Annie's head he could almost see one or two of them doing a fast mental count. Who cared? His wife was going to have a baby!

''Congratulations,'' said his secretary, rising as he reentered his office with his arm around Annie. She grinned. ''We'll finish this later.''

He nodded, his attention on his wife. *His pregnant wife!* Delight streaked through him, followed immediately by concern for Annie. ''How are you feeling? What did the doctor say? When is the baby due?''

"Whoa!" She held up a hand in self-defense, ticking off her answers on her fingers. "I feel okay...for the moment. I didn't see the doctor, but I did speak with a nurse who made an appointment for my first checkup in four weeks. And—" she looked momentarily bewildered "—I don't know when the baby is due!"

Dane laughed again. "Well, I can probably give you a rough estimate, seeing as how I was in on the creation of this little miracle." He kissed her, then kissed her again more deeply when she responded to him the way she always did, her body curling into his, the fine electricity they generated together zipping through him, stirring male instincts and male flesh in unmistakable signs of desire.

He damn near forgot where he was when she did that. Letting her go, he hooked his foot around a chair. "Here, sit down. You shouldn't be on your feet any more than you have to be."

Annie's eyes slowly focused and sharpened with amusement. "Don't tell me you're going to be a worrywart. Women have been having babies for centuries and a lot of them worked harder than I ever will." She dropped a sheaf of papers and pamphlets on his desk. "This is all about early nutrition and fetal development and exercise and birthing class options—you name it, I have it. Here."

She handed him a little cardboard square with a movable wheel attached to it. "You wanted to know our due date. That'll tell us."

Intrigued, he flipped the little gadget over and read the directions on the back, then looked over it at her.

"Okay. When was your last...oh." He felt rather foolish. "You haven't had...since...it was that first time, wasn't it?"

She nodded, blushing only faintly. "I think so."

He knelt beside the chair. "That means we're going to be parents in—" he consulted the little wheel "—July."

"July." She whispered the word as if it were a prayer.

He looked at her shining eyes. "You are the most marvelous woman in the world," he said, putting his arms around her again. "I can't believe I found you."

Annie floated through the next few days on a cloud of happiness heightened by Dane's delight in her condition. The spotting had stopped just as the nurse had indicated it would and she didn't tell him about it at all.

Jeanne called and they hashed over physical symptoms, baby names and labor and delivery information. Annie started a list, at Jeanne's urging, of all the things she and Dane would need for the baby.

She continued to feel queasy in the evenings. She discovered that if she ate like a horse in the morning and didn't eat anything after about two p.m., the nausea was mild enough for her to get through her early-evening classes. She enlisted one of her most experienced dog handlers to oversee the three late classes on Tuesday, Wednesday and Friday and temporarily stopped attending the Thursday-night meetings of the canine club. Fortunately, her eight-week Basic classes had just graduated and wouldn't resume until January.

One evening after she came home from her late class, Dane came into the den where she was lying on the couch watching an early edition of the news.

"How are you feeling?" he asked, settling himself on the edge of the cushions, against her hip.

"Pretty good. Maybe my hormones are adjusting at last." She smiled at him, loving the solicitous manner with which he treated her. It might only be because she was carrying his child, but it allowed her to pretend that she was special to him, that he cared about *her* rather than simply about her condition.

"I have an ulterior motive," he warned her.

"Oh?" Her expression was full of coy innocence. She placed her hand over his where it rested lightly on her abdomen. He'd made love to her often since they'd learned about the baby, but he'd been as careful and gentle as if she were made of the most fragile porcelain. She found she missed the rough, urgent mastery with which he'd taken her before he learned about the baby.

"Not that," he said indulgently. "Though I'm not saying the idea doesn't have merit."

She grinned, feeling sassy. "I thought it was a pretty good idea, myself. But what's your 'ulterior motive'?"

Dane's face lost its contentment. "I have to go out for dinner next Tuesday evening. Business meeting I couldn't wriggle out of."

Since he'd learned of her pregnancy, he'd rarely gone out in the evening.

"That's okay." And it was. She'd miss spending time with him, but she didn't want to interfere with his job.

"Trouble is, the guy's bringing his wife. I told him you worked on Tuesday evenings, but I think he was expecting me to try to get you to join us."

She was silent. What did he want her to say? Was he expecting her to cancel her classes or get a substitute? Guilt rose. She had known when she married him that she wasn't the kind of wife he needed. "I'm sorry I can't join you," she said in a near whisper.

"Annie, look at me." Dane's voice was firm and she realized she'd been avoiding his gaze. "Don't be sorry. I wouldn't have told you at all but I didn't want you to worry about where I was or who I was with." He turned his hand over beneath hers and squeezed it. "Actually, I wish I had your excuse. The guy's a crotchety old geezer and I'd have begged off if he weren't on the board of directors."

*On the board of directors!* She felt worse than ever, but he was clearly trying to make her feel better and she didn't want him to worry. "Sounds like I'm getting off lucky." She took his hand and carried it to her breast. "Now that that's out of the way, what were we discussing?"

"I don't remember." But his hand moved to shape her breast as if he couldn't help himself.

She stretched, enjoying the beginnings of arousal produced by the warmth and nearness of him and the stroking sensation at her breast, putting her fears into the back of her mind. "Is it coming back to you yet?"

"It is. Are you sure it's okay?" At her nod, his blue eyes grew intense and heavy-lidded. "Hold that thought." In one quick, smooth motion, he was on his feet, calling the dogs. They staggered up from their relaxed positions on the floor near Annie and he called them to their crates on the enclosed porch.

"Sorry, girls," she heard him say to them. "There are just some times when a cold, wet nose isn't lovable."

He turned around after he closed the back door, planning to retrace his steps through the darkened kitchen to rejoin Annie in the den. But as he moved, he bumped squarely into her standing right behind him. He automatically thrust out his hands to catch her and she stepped into his arms, pressing herself against him and lifting her face for his kiss.

He was more than willing to oblige. His body responded immediately to the feel of her warm curves and he slipped his hands under her bottom and lifted her, fitting her more intimately against him. He thrust his tongue into her mouth, kissing her deeply for long minutes, then he trailed his lips across her cheek and lifted his head to inspect her face in the shadows.

If she knew what it did to him when she got that dreamy, absorbed expression on her face, she'd have an incredibly powerful weapon at her disposal. He was impatient to touch her, too impatient to carry her all the way upstairs. Pivoting, he set her down on the edge of the counter, freeing his hands to deal with the tiny buttons that ran down the front of her blouse. He couldn't wait to touch those beautiful breasts. As the blouse parted beneath his fingers, he realized she had pulled it free from her skirt and started working the buttons open from the bottom. That aroused him even more and he became supremely aware of his hardened flesh pressing against her through the barriers of their clothing. He was standing between her legs, which she had wrapped around his hips when he set her on the counter. He surged once against her, a temporary cure for what ailed him, and then she was yanking her blouse and bra off and pulling his head down toward the tempting mounds of creamy flesh, tipped with hard buttons which were little more than darker-colored shadows in the dim room.

She was driving him crazy! Although Annie never failed to excite him beyond reason, she had been a fairly passive lover throughout the recent weeks of their passion, letting him take the lead. She was so beautifully responsive that he hadn't realized until now that she had never displayed any aggression in their lovemaking. Her frantic need to have him touching her breasts inflamed him even more and he groaned as he palmed the cool slopes, lifting one ivory mound to suck strongly at its peak.

She gasped and arched toward him, damp hands tunneling through his hair to pull him even closer. He continued to suckle her and the ache in his loins grew to an enormous throbbing. Rocking her buttocks from side to side, she shifted repeatedly over his stiffened shaft. Her hands moved from his hair to tear in haste at the buttons of his shirt, tugging it out of the way and pulling his undershirt up underneath his arms so that she could touch the muscled planes of skin covered with whorls of black curls. She found his nipples and brushed her thumbs over them until they were as hard and tight as her own.

He hadn't intended for it to go this far this fast but the need that rose to claw at him like a living thing wouldn't be appeased. Forgetting their surroundings, he lifted handfuls of her cotton skirt out of his way until all that remained between her legs was a swatch of lacy panties. He tugged them swiftly down, moving away only long enough to remove them altogether and then he was back, the tender skin of her inner thighs deliciously hot and exciting against the exposed flesh of his belly.

Unable to resist the lure of her satin heat, he trailed his fingers down over her warm, soft belly, not yet swollen with the evidence of his child growing within her. Soft flesh gave way to a cloud of silky curls shielding the very heart of her desire; with a groan, he curled his fingers farther down, tracing her repeatedly until moisture slicked the humid flesh beneath his questing fingertips.

She was like an untamed mare in his arms, twisting and plunging as he entered her with nothing more than his fingers and he caught her sobs of breath in his own hungry mouth. Her hands slipped down between them and he felt her ripping at his belt and the fastenings of his pants... then glorious freedom as his erect manhood burst free of the confining cloth. She surrounded him with hot, silken fingers before he could draw in enough oxygen to protest, to halt her before she sent him over the edge of the chasm on which his self-control was precariously perched—and then it was too late. He could only groan deep in his throat as she caressed him at a steadily increasing pace, throwing his head back and clenching his teeth as her thumb slicked over the tip of his straining flesh, spreading the moisture that she found there.

Like someone demented, he quickly tore her hands away, feeling the end overtaking him in great bursts of thrusting power. He was out of control as he grasped her slim hips and lifted her onto him, exhaling in relief as he felt her warm, tight depths accept him totally, taking his pent-up pulsations as he spilled his seed. At the same time, he pushed her body to a quivering crescendo that had her screaming before she arched repeatedly into his big body in her own shivering, pulsing climax.

As his body relaxed, occasional frissons of aftershock quaked through him. His legs abruptly felt like jelly and he slid to the floor, still holding her against him. He collapsed flat on his back and she fell forward, using his massive proportions as a pillow.

Neither of them stirred for a long moment. Finally, Annie drew in a deep breath and exhaled. "Shall we sleep here?"

He snorted. "Easy for you to say. I'm the one lying on the floor." He raised a large hand and caressed her bottom gently. "Let's go to bed."

Dane had gone downstairs to let the dogs out when she awoke the next morning. She turned on her side and hugged his pillow to her. Until recently, she'd been an early riser. Now Dane made breakfast for her instead of the other way around. The exhaustion she'd heard so much about was taking its toll on her and she often went back to sleep again after he left in the morning. Her bladder also was letting her know that her body was changing, she thought in resigned amusement as she threw back the covers.

It wasn't until she went into the bathroom that she discovered she was spotting again. And the blood was a bright, frightening red this time.

Terror seized her. Jeanne had never mentioned anything like this, so it couldn't be normal. She wanted this baby so much—was she losing it? And Dane. He would be devastated.

Coming back out of the bathroom, she threw on her clothing. The doctor's office opened at eight and she intended to be there.

Dane came in as she was slipping on her shoes. "Wow! She stirs." Then he caught sight of her face. "Honey, what's the matter?"

She read in his eyes all the fear she was feeling as she told him about the spotting.

"Do you think we...what we did...hurt it?"

"I don't know," she answered miserably. "It shouldn't have. The nurse told me intercourse was fine."

"I'm coming to the doctor's with you."

It was a little thing, but having him with her made her feel so much better. They arrived at the office promptly at eight and when Annie explained the problem, they were shown directly into an examining room. After the examination, the doctor, whom she'd used since she was married to Nick, was matter-of-fact.

"I don't feel much enlargement in the uterus but that's not unusual this early in a pregnancy, especially if we've miscalculated the due date and you're not as far along as we think."

"But is the bleeding normal?" Dane cut right to what was worrying her, as well.

The doctor hesitated. "It's not necessarily *abnormal,* although continued spotting wouldn't be a good sign." He pulled Annie's sweater down gently and helped her to sit up on the examining table. "Right now there isn't much we can do except wait. The first trimester is the time when the embryo is establishing itself in the womb. If there is any reason for that not to happen, this is when it occurs. It's simply Nature's way of ensuring that most babies born are healthy and normal."

"So we should just wait?"

The doctor smiled. "I said there's little we can do, not nothing. I want you—" he turned to Annie "—to stay off your feet as much as possible. Rest until you think you can't stand to stay in bed another minute, lie on a couch if you can. If you have to get up, find a chair as soon as possible. And no exercise. No walking, even."

Annie was stunned. What about her business . . . ? But she wouldn't take even the smallest chance if it might endanger the baby. "All right."

The doctor nodded approvingly. "Let's hope a little extra rest will set everything right. But if you have any more spotting, even a tiny bit, contact me immediately. We'll set up an ultrasound to see what's going on in there."

She felt much better after talking to the doctor, although her head was whirling with the arrangements she'd have to make with the canine center. Dane drove her home and settled her on the couch. He'd called in to the bank to tell them he was taking the morning off.

As he returned from the kitchen with a large glass of water and a plate of grapes and vegetables he'd prepared for her, she said, "This will speed up my timetable for scaling back the business, but the more I think about it, the more comfortable I feel with it."

"Scaling back the business . . . ?" he echoed.

"Yes." She smiled and shrugged. "I'd have had to do it when the baby was born, anyway."

Dane set the glass on a coaster and settled himself on the edge of the sofa. "Annie, are you sure you want to do this?" His eyes were very blue and his handsome features were set in serious lines. "I don't expect you to give up anything you don't want to. I know we haven't talked about it, but I assumed we might hire someone to care for the baby when both of us were working, maybe even a live-in nanny. For that matter, we could hire someone who would go with you to work so the baby could be near you." He placed his hands on her shoulders. "I want you to be happy."

*How can I be happy without your love?* It was the first thought that flashed through her mind and she immediately dropped her gaze from his, afraid he might read the naked longing there. She shouldn't be discontented, she lectured herself. Dane might not love her but he cared about her. They had a good, solid marriage and this baby was something that delighted them both.

"I am happy," she said softly. "This baby means so much to me. I don't want to be one of those career mothers who barely sees her infant. I want to be there for all those firsts." She placed her hands on his strong forearms. "I enjoy what I've created with the canine center, but I'm going to enjoy being a mother more."

Dane's expression relaxed. "You sound like you mean it."

"I do!"

"I know that now. I didn't want you to think I expected you to give up something you loved."

Inside her, a wall gave way. The insecurities that had plagued her since the earliest days of her first marriage, the fears that she wasn't the right kind of wife for a man whose business included an ability to socialize, were swept away on a rising tide of understanding.

Dane truly didn't consider her to be a social negative. He wanted her to be happy. He didn't care what kind of work she did or if she even worked at all. And he was sure that she wouldn't be a burden to his career, or he wouldn't be so insistent in his determination to be sure she was making the right decision with her canine center.

On Tuesday of next week, she was lying on the couch with her feet up when Dane came through the door.

"Hello." She barely got the greeting out before he leaned down to kiss her. Immediately, she forgot all about anything else she'd planned to say as his lips molded hers in sweet demand. It was going to be a long four weeks, she thought, until the next checkup. One of the additional things the doctor had recommended they do was suspend their lovemaking until her next checkup.

"Hello." He pulled his head back a fraction. "I missed you today."

Her heart leaped at the husky words. "I missed you, too." She knew he was frustrated by their circumstances from the hungry kisses he gave her every evening, but for the first time, she allowed herself to hope for something more. Could it be possible that he was beginning to love her the way she loved him?

As he slipped an arm under her back and another under her knees, she circled his neck with her arms. "It's not time for bed yet. Where are you taking me?"

"I have something to show you." He carried her effortlessly through the kitchen, onto the back porch and out to the driveway.

"Where's your car?" She was confused. In the driveway, where he usually parked the little white sports car, was a burgundy sedan. The metallic finish gleamed and she saw that it was so new the price sheet was still tacked to the window. "What's this?"

He laughed. "A car. Our car, to be precise. Like it?"

"But..." She still didn't get it. "What happened to the Jaguar?"

"I traded it in," he said promptly.

"What?" She twisted in his arms to stare at him. "But, Dane, you loved that car! Why did you trade it for this?"

He laughed and kissed her forehead. "Don't worry on my account, sweetheart. I did enjoy owning the

Jag, but it was just a car. We need a family car now in addition to the van." He walked toward the pretty vehicle. "Want to sit in the driver's seat and check it out?"

As he set her gently on the burgundy leather seat, he kissed her again, lingering for a moment to nuzzle her cheek.

Regret seeped through her. "I'm sorry we can't—I can't—would you like me to...? Oh, forget it!"

"It's okay," he said softly, smiling at her embarrassment. "I enjoy kissing and touching you. It doesn't mean we have to make love each time I do. I can wait until you're with me again."

The hope grew a little stronger within her breast. Even though they'd married for reasons that had nothing to do with love, there was a chance that their marriage could lead to love. The words nearly charged out of her mouth then, *I love you*. But she held them back. She didn't want to make him feel uncomfortable. And they had the rest of their lives to share their love.

# Eight

Another week passed. She hired additional help at the dog center and planned to cut back the courses offered in the winter session. She already rented the building to the Dog Guide Puppy Club and a local cat fanciers club on a monthly basis, but she ran an ad in the paper to attract other groups who might be hunting for a meeting place. Although the classes she was keeping would still cover her expenses, she hated to see the building stand empty much of the time.

The following Saturday, Dane carried her down to the couch, which had become her regular resting place. He allowed her to sit up for a while in the morning since she'd been lying flat all night and she propped her feet up as the doctor had requested. Dane immediately left the room, and she assumed he'd gone to make breakfast. But he returned with a folder, which he dropped in her lap. "Here. Look through these while I get us some breakfast." He grinned and winked at her as he turned to leave.

Wondering what had produced his high spirits, she opened the folder. Several catalogs spilled out. Catalogs? Curious now, she picked up one and noticed immediately that the corners of several pages were turned down. Flipping to one, she discovered that it was the beginning of a section on cribs and nursery furniture. Another displayed a new product that automatically sealed dirty diapers in a small plastic package. And a third page contained descriptions of accent pieces in nursery motifs, lamps, switch plates and bookends that all matched a theme.

She laughed aloud and began to study the pages with real interest. Had there ever been a more excited father-to-be?

"See anything you like?" Dane came into the room again, carrying a tray set with breakfast for two. Placing it on the coffee table, he carefully sank down next to her and placed his arm around her.

She snuggled closer, feeling cherished. "Lots. How about you?"

"I haven't looked too much," he admitted. "But I thought that since you can't go shopping, we could decide what we wanted this way and order it."

They debated and decided, argued and agreed during the next two hours. Annie was shocked at the amount of baby equipment and furniture Dane seemed prepared to buy without batting an eyelash.

"I don't want this baby to lack anything," was all he said when she protested.

"Babies have been raised all over the world with far less than this," she responded with stubborn reason. "Children need love and attention, not *things*."

He only shrugged, refusing to rise to her bait. "Then this kid will have it all, because we already know he's going to be cuddled every waking moment of our time, anyway."

"But...I really think *this* is an unnecessary expense," she said, pointing to the three infant seats he'd selected. "One is plenty. I don't need one for downstairs, one for upstairs and one for the dog center. I'll probably forget they're there and carry one from place to place, anyway."

He eyed her, clearly measuring her determination. Then he sighed. "I guess I am going a little overboard, aren't I?"

"A little?" She gave him a dry look.

"I'm sorry, but this is important to me." His tone was defensive. "You don't know what it's like to grow up as a child watching other kids get all kinds of things from their parents. My kid isn't going to learn to ride a bike on an old secondhand that's already been through two families."

Annie bit her lip, deciding not to point out that babies couldn't tell if something wasn't brand-spanking new. Dane rarely talked about himself. In fact, he retreated from the subject when she tried to introduce it. This opportunity was too welcome to miss. "I know it's important to you," she said, and waited.

"Damned right it is." He got up from the couch in a single, restless movement and began to pace around

the room. "My kids are never going to wonder what
it would be like to be loved."

Her heart ached for him. She understood now. This
buying spree wasn't about making sure his child had
the biggest and the best on the block. It was simply
overcompensation—Dane's answer to blocking any
chance of his child's feeling the neglect that had stung
him throughout his own formative years. In some way,
creating this family and doing all the things he'd
longed for as a child would give him a measure of
peace from his past.

How could she deny him that? In retrospect, her
concerns about spending seemed small. "All right,"
she said. "As long as our checkbook doesn't whim-
per when we open it, you can get whatever you like."

He looked at her strangely. "But I don't want to get
whatever I like. I want you to be involved in this, to
help me make decisions." His face hardened. "I already had one wife who didn't care about half the decisions I made, I don't need another."

She didn't speak. This time she didn't know what to
say. After a moment, it was as if he couldn't stand the
expectant silence.

"Amanda only bothered to argue with me when she
was directly affected by whatever I wanted to do. Like
have a child."

"She didn't want children?"

The corners of his mouth turned down. "Not mine.
Oh, she said she did when we got married. But when I
started to press the issue, she balked." His eyes narrowed and Annie was glad she wasn't the one of whom
he spoke. "She stalled me for months, for over two

years. We finally had it out one night and she admitted she didn't want to be tied down with a child. Ever."

There was a short silence.

She couldn't imagine any woman crazy enough not to want Dane's baby. "And so you got divorced," she said with soft sympathy.

He snorted and it was full of an ugly self-mockery. His voice was bitter as he said, "I left her for a few months. To think things through. But I'm not a quitter and I decided to try again, to give her more time and see if we couldn't work things out." He raised his gaze to hers and she almost recoiled at the rage banked behind his eyes. "But when I went home, she had already found a replacement for me. And she was pregnant with his child."

Annie gasped. She closed her eyes against the bleak pain in his gaze. She wanted to reach for him, to offer comfort but she knew from the rigid set of his shoulders that he wouldn't accept it from her.

His story explained so much. And as his words sank in, her heart shriveled into a small ball of pain. She'd been so sure that eventually she could win his love. But Dane wasn't about to allow himself to love her, or anyone. He wouldn't even accept her comfort.

And why should he? She wasn't someone he loved. After what he'd been through, he wasn't going to open himself up to that kind of hurt again. Understanding didn't make it any easier to realize that her dream of being loved by him was no more than that—a dream.

With her heart a leaden weight in her chest, she turned to the next item on their list.

Another disquieting thought wormed its way into her mind, but she didn't have the courage to ask him if her primary qualification for becoming his wife had been her willingness to bear children. Actually, she knew she didn't have the courage to hear the answer.

They decided on nursery furnishings and he set the information aside. He would order everything on Monday. Right now, he wanted to concentrate on Annie. She'd been even quieter than usual throughout the afternoon and evening and she'd pleaded fatigue at an early hour.

When he carried her to bed, he could feel the resistance in her small body and he realized with a shock that whatever was eating at her had something to do with him. But a mental review of his behavior, of their recent conversations gave him no clue as to why she might be upset with him.

"Is something the matter?" he asked once she was tucked into her side of their big bed for the night.

"What could be the matter?" But she wouldn't meet his eyes.

A chill invaded his system. He'd never realized how much he needed Annie's unquestioning warmth and approval, her silent support and sweet caring. Until now, when she seemed to be withholding it.

Didn't she realize how much he needed her? Determined not to let her create distance between them, he bent forward and set his lips to hers. She didn't resist him, but she didn't respond, either. Softly he molded the contours of her mouth until she allowed him to part her lips and seek the sweetness inside. He increased the intensity of the kiss gradually, pulling her up against his chest and kissing her deeply until she grasped his biceps and moaned in protest.

Almost immediately, he remembered her condition. "I'm sorry, sweetheart," he murmured gently, placing his lips against her forehead for a last caress. "I miss making love to you. I can't wait until this baby is born."

"I can't, either," she said, and he was relieved to see the trusting warmth back in her gaze again.

He went downstairs to let the dogs in and crate them for the night, and when he came back to bed, she was already asleep, curled on her side with one hand under her cheek, palm up. Warm feeling surged through him as he crawled into bed beside her and curled protectively around her.

His wife. Mother of his child. He'd take care of her.

It was still dark when the groaning woke him. The bedside clock read five-twenty a.m. Disoriented, he sat up and switched on the light. His confusion turned quickly to panic as he realized what he'd heard was Annie crying.

She was still on her side, but now she was doubled up, with her knees drawn up. As he bent over her, she moaned.

"Annie! Sweetheart, what's wrong?" His heart leaped into his throat.

"Dane." Tears leaked from the corners of her eyes. "Something's wrong. I . . . hurt. Call the doctor."

He threw two blankets over her as he punched the buttons of the telephone. The answering service had to locate the doctor and have him return the call, and he sweated out the minutes that seemed like hours passing, letting her squeeze his hand when pain rolled through her, fear turning his big body into a shaking frame of flesh.

When the telephone rang, he pounced on it. Annie's doctor listened to Dane's stumbling explanation, then asked him to bring her to the hospital. Daylight was just beginning to touch the night sky with streaks of rose and ivory as he carried her slight weight in his arms through the doors of the emergency entrance.

In an examining room, the doctor palpated her stomach, then raised sober eyes to Dane. "I want to do an ultrasound immediately. She doesn't seem to be developing as she should be for a woman who is about nine weeks along."

"What do you think the trouble is?" Dane felt frantic, his attention divided between the doctor and Annie, who was grinding her teeth in pain now.

But the doctor refused to speculate. "Let's see what the ultrasound shows us."

Things moved rapidly after that. Paperwork had to be completed and orderlies came in to help Annie out of her clothes and into a regulation hospital gown. They brought her liquids to drink and asked her to drink as much as she could. Before Dane knew it, they were placing Annie on a stretcher and carrying her to another part of the hospital.

"Will I be allowed to stay with her?" He kept pace with Annie on the stretcher as the orderlies moved down the hall, still holding her hand.

"Sure." The technician who met them again outside the door of the room where the test would occur, took a moment to pat him on the shoulder. "The calmer you are, the more you can help your wife, Mr. Hamilton."

*Calm!* As they positioned Annie on the table and set the machine in place, he wanted to scream aloud. This was his wife in pain and they wanted him to be calm. Belatedly, it occurred to him that she could be losing the baby, but he refused to allow himself to dwell on that fear. If this didn't work out, they could always try again. The important thing was that they help Annie.

The test seemed to take forever. He watched the screen that displayed the contents of Annie's insides, but none of it was identifiable. He helped Annie to the bathroom as soon as the ultrasound was finished and waited anxiously outside the door until she came out, still in the grip of the pain that seemed to be clawing at her abdomen.

"It doesn't feel like labor," she panted as they helped her back onto the table and she lay down. "I always imagined labor to come in waves. This—just hurts."

He could hear the technician and the doctor conferring in low tones and then the doctor came into the room.

"Mr. and Mrs. Hamilton, the ultrasound shows an ectopic pregnancy." He must have read their blank expressions correctly because he continued. "What that means is that the fertilized egg attached to the inside of one fallopian tube rather than traveling on into the womb where it needs to be to grow to term. Mrs.

Hamilton will need immediate surgery to remove the embryo. As it grows, it becomes too large for the tube until the tube ruptures. The pain you're having is probably a warning of that very thing. If the tube ruptures, the condition can be fatal to the mother as well as the baby."

"So we're going to lose the baby?" It was his own voice, Dane knew, but it sounded like some weary stranger's.

The doctor nodded, his eyes full of grave sympathy. "I'm afraid so."

"But Dr. Milner—" Annie's tones were full of choked urgency. "What will this do to our chances of having more children?"

The doctor hesitated. "I can't really address that just yet, Mrs. Hamilton. If we are able to save the tube, the possibility exists that future pregnancies could occur, but scar tissue often forms in these situations. We just don't know. I have to warn you that the prognosis for keeping the tube intact in these cases is usually very poor."

*The prognosis is very poor.* The words battered themselves against his brain, slowly sorting themselves into an awful truth. Because of the accident, this was the only functioning fallopian tube Annie possessed. If this one was damaged or destroyed by the misplaced pregnancy, she wouldn't be able to conceive his child.

Too late he realized he'd been silent for too long. He looked down into Annie's eyes and saw instantly that she was realizing the death of their dreams, as well.

Her small face was pinched and gray and in her eyes welled the tears of a bleak defeat that broke his heart.

Leaning down, he slipped his arms around her slender shoulders, hugging her to him while his own eyes stung. Not for the first time, it hit him how tiny and fragile she really was. His protective instincts kicked into gear. Reassuring Annie was his first and most important task. Later, when he was alone, he could examine how this would affect him.

"The doctor's going to take care of you," he said against her hair. "I'm sorry about the baby, but it isn't the end of the world." Two orderlies approached then, to take her away in preparation for the surgery. He bent down to kiss her lips. They were cold, and up close he could read the anguish in her eyes so clearly that he wanted to cry. "I'll be waiting for you," he said, though he could hardly get the words out for the tears that threatened to choke off his voice.

He called Patrick immediately, and Joe and Jeanne Krynes, as well. Within an hour, all of them descended on the waiting room where he was sitting in a state of numb anxiety.

When he told them the doctor's bleak assessment, Jeanne turned her face into Joe's shoulder in tears. One hand went to her own abdomen and Dane knew she was sharing their loss. Joe clasped Dane's shoulder briefly and Dane saw the glimmer of moisture in the other man's eyes.

Patrick turned away, staring out the window for long minutes until Dane joined him. He felt raw and sick inside with grief, but Patrick was Annie's brother, someone she loved, and he knew he had to try to comfort him.

Patrick's hands were clenched on the protruding edge of the windowsill when Dane stepped to his side. He was staring out the window with narrowed eyes, but Dane doubted he could have told anyone what was outside. He slung an arm around Patrick's broad shoulders. "You doing all right?"

The shoulders beneath his arm slumped. "It just isn't fair." Patrick's voice was dull with pain. "She's had enough rotten lumps in her life. I've felt so good lately, so damned good because she seemed happy again—" He stopped, turning to Dane with an appalled expression. "God, Dane, I'm sorry. I should be the one listening to you."

Dane shrugged. "It's okay. You've been a rock of strength for her for a lot of years. It makes sense that this would be hard to take."

Patrick's eyes, as blue and deep as Annie's, searched his face. "I know you two were really excited about the baby." His face changed to sorrow. "And to find out at the same time that there may not be any more . . . that's tough. How are you doing?"

Dane hesitated. He did feel grief for the little life that wasn't to be. But he was more concerned about Annie. "I'm okay," he said roughly. "Or I will be as soon as somebody tells me Annie came through all right."

Just then someone pushed the double doors from the surgery wing, interrupting their conversation. When Dane recognized the doctor who'd operated on

Annie, he moved across the room like a shot from a cannon. "How's my wife?"

The doctor nodded. "She's stable and doing pretty well. Right now she's in the recovery room. As soon as she can be moved back to her room, you can see her."

"What are her chances of having more children?" This time Patrick spoke. He put an arm around Dane's shoulder as if to brace him.

The doctor switched his gaze to Dane, and he read the answer there before the man spoke. "I'm sorry, Mr. Hamilton, we couldn't save the tube. It had sustained significant damage. Your wife still has one intact ovary, but she won't be able to conceive the conventional way."

Behind him, Jeanne began to sob. The doctor looked both helpless and defeated. "I'm sorry," he said again. "If you check at the desk, they'll direct you to the recovery room. You should be able to see her soon."

Annie was going to be all right. Dane started down the hallway, oblivious to the presence of the others behind him. He hoped they would let him see her soon because he thought he might tear the place apart otherwise. He had a lot to tell her.

Regretfully, he thought of the children they might have had together, girls with blue eyes and their mother's mahogany tresses, boys... It didn't matter any more. His dream of children could never be realized. And he didn't even care.

*He loved her.* He'd loved her for months and he hadn't even told her. Thank God she was going to be all right. Thank God he'd have the chance to tell her how much she meant to him.

He was waiting in her room when they wheeled her in, and as soon as all the hovering attendants had left, he stepped forward and took her hand. "Hi, sweetheart."

She rolled her head toward him. "Hi."

He was shocked by the lifeless quality of her voice. Maybe it was the result of the anesthesia. Though he'd planned to tell her how he felt right away, he just couldn't tell her now. He leaned forward to kiss her forehead.

She rolled her head away again and his kiss landed somewhere near her temple. Tears seeped from the corners of her eyes.

"Honey, don't. Please, don't." He felt helpless and panicky as he gently blotted the tears with the corner of the sheet. "Try to rest and we'll talk when you wake up."

She did drift off into a restless sleep. Three times the nurses came in to check her vital signs and she allowed them to poke and prod, then closed her eyes and slipped back into whatever dream world she was inhabiting. Several times she woke, nauseated, but a few sips of carbonated soda seemed to help. The nurses told him it was probably the effects of the anesthesia and that she'd feel better tomorrow.

Around four o'clock a meal came. Annie was in no shape to eat it and he suddenly realized he hadn't had a meal since dinner the night before. As he finished wolfing down the cardboard hospital food, he realized Annie had awakened and was watching him.

He smiled at her. "Welcome back. I thought you were going to sleep around the clock."

"I wish I hadn't woken up at all. I lost the baby, didn't I?"

He hesitated, then nodded. The sorrow in her eyes broke his heart anew. "Sweetheart, I'm sorry. I feel badly about our baby, too. But you're going to be fine."

"Am I?" Her voice was dull. "Will I be able to have more children?"

He hesitated again.

The slight pause was fatal. Her shoulders shook as she turned her head away again.

"Annie..." He sank on to the side of the bed, mindful of not jolting her incision, and stroked his hand from the ball of her shoulder down her arm and back again in a comforting gesture. "Children would have been nice...but that's not what's most important to me." He picked up her limp hand and squeezed it. "You're what I care most about. If we don't have children...we'll be all right."

She went still but she didn't turn to face him.

What had he expected? He knew he'd phrased it badly, but he'd thought she'd at least acknowledge his words. He opened his mouth, then shut it again. Maybe his timing was just lousy.

But old hurts rose to taunt him. If she loved him, wouldn't she have responded when he tried to reassure her?

*If she loved him...* The great vein of insecurity that had been buried in his heart since Amanda had refused to have his baby lay exposed, clogging his thought with its poisonous residue. Annie had never said she loved him, even though he'd thought she did, had *hoped* she did. All his life he'd looked for love, had longed for someone to whom he was the first light in the sky and the last ray at sunset. He'd stood on the outside all through his childhood, longing for a love like that.

When he'd met Amanda, he'd wanted it so much that in his mind he'd made their relationship something deeper, more meaningful than it ever was in reality. And when she'd shattered his heart, he'd thought he would never recover. But Annie had stolen into his life and his heart—

And he'd thought she loved him. It looked as if he'd been wrong again.

He studied her pale profile for a moment longer, but still she didn't acknowledge his presence or his words in any way. Slowly, he took his hands from her and got to his feet. As he made his way from the room, the remains of his heart slid to the floor and shattered into a thousand shards.

Five days later, Annie was released from the hospital. Simply walking from the car into the living room exhausted her and she sank into a chair in the den and accepted Ebony's and Missy's exuberant licks. Their unquestioning joy cheered her a little, but only for a short time.

"Can I get you something?" Dane paused in the doorway after taking her suitcase upstairs. He looked handsome and worried, self-contained and...

unapproachable. As he had since the first day after surgery.

"No, thank you. I'll be fine. Jeanne said she'd check in at lunchtime so you won't have to come home."

He hesitated. "All right. If you're sure you don't need me...."

"I'll be fine." *If only you knew how much I need you!* But he'd already vanished from the doorway and she heard the back door close quietly as he left for work. She heard the engine of the new family sedan he'd bought a week earlier purr to life and then he was gone.

And she dropped her head and let the tears fall.

She hadn't cried in the hospital since that first day, when she'd realized how much she'd lost. Too little privacy. And she hadn't wanted Dane to walk in and see her crying. It wasn't his fault this had happened.

It wasn't her fault, either. But she knew the loss of this baby and the impossibility of conceiving again spelled the loss of her dreams of love and the end of her marriage.

The tears fell faster as she thought of how noble he'd been the day of the surgery. *You're what I care most about....* But he hadn't said he loved her. The omission was telling.

It had broken her heart to realize his words had been prompted by nothing more than pity. She'd been too busy trying not to sob aloud to tell him he didn't have to pretend. And she hadn't been able to look at his beloved face knowing that he didn't really love her as she loved him.

# Nine

Jeanne came over close to lunchtime. She had an oddly hesitant manner about her and to Annie's surprise, she lingered on the back doorstep until Annie invited her in.

"What's the matter with you?" Annie asked. "Any other day you'd barge right in. You don't have to act different just because I'm married."

Jeanne tried a smile that wobbled around the edges. "It isn't that. I was afraid—I mean, if you can't bear to see me, I'll go away."

It was true that Annie had been trying to pretend she didn't notice the bulge of early pregnancy under Jeanne's loose shirt. The baby was due in May, just weeks before her own baby would have arrived.

She sighed, reaching for Jeanne's hand even as her eyes filled. "Get in here, you fool."

Jeanne came forward with her arms outstretched and Annie stepped into her embrace. They stayed like that for a long moment until the tears were under control. Feeling the hard mound of Jeanne's abdomen pressed against her was a bittersweet sorrow but Annie forced herself not to think about it. Stepping back, she said, "I'm not going to be able to avoid seeing pregnant women and babies for the rest of my life, you know."

"I know." Jeanne wiped her own tears before slinging her coat and purse across one of the kitchen chairs. "I wasn't sure you were ready to be confronted with someone else's pregnancy just yet."

Annie nodded, unable to deny it as she turned away to make tea.

Jeanne pulled out a chair. She placed a tea bag in the mug Annie offered her and propped her feet on a chair opposite the one in which she sat. Changing the topic, she regaled Annie with the latest news from around the community.

By the time they'd finished the tea, it was lunchtime.

"Don't get up," Jeanne warned Annie as she rose. "You're supposed to be recuperating, remember? I brought lunch along." She opened the picnic hamper she'd brought with her and began to set out the meal she'd put together.

They ate while they continued to talk, though Annie noticed Jeanne studiously skirted any talk of child rearing or childbearing. Maybe by the next time Jeanne visited, Annie would feel up to asking the normal questions and discussing babies, but today she was grateful for the omission.

As Jeanne repacked her things in the basket, though, she gazed across the table at Annie seriously and her hands stilled. "How's Dane taking this?"

The question caught her flat-footed. To her horror, Annie felt the tears well again. "All right," she managed to say, swallowing. "He'll be fi—" But the dam broke and more of the tears that she'd suppressed in the hospital sprang up, swamping her in the misery that was breaking her heart.

Jeanne's face registered distress. In a flash, she was around the table and pulling a chair close so she could cradle Annie in her arms. "Oh, honey, I could tell by the way he watched J.J. and Mindy—as if he could just cuddle them to bits—that he longed for kids of his own. Has he been terribly upset?"

Annie only shook her head.

Jeanne rocked her, snagging a napkin from the table and drying Annie's tears herself.

This was what she needed, Annie thought bleakly. But instead of receiving comfort from her husband, she was dependent on the charity of others. With a final sniff, she forced herself to sit up and stop leaning on Jeanne. Quietly, she said, "I don't know if Dane's been upset or not. We're not communicating well these days."

Jeanne said nothing but her expression held dismay.

Annie continued before she lost her nerve. "Dane only married me because we both wanted children and this was a convenient solution. Now that I can't conceive, I imagine he'll want out of the marriage." Her voice quavered on the last two words but she bit down on the inside of her lip until the pain was stronger than the agony tearing at her heart.

Jeanne snorted. "That's nonsense. Dane loves you. He's not going to leave you just because you've had a rotten break."

"No, you don't understand." Annie shook her head emphatically. "I knew when we got married that the most important thing in his life was becoming a father."

"Are you trying to tell me there was no love involved in your marriage?" Jeanne sounded wary and disbelieving.

"Not on his part." She gave the pregnant woman a weary smile. "I'm sure my feelings for him are no secret, but he doesn't—"

"Bull."

Annie stared at her. "What?"

Jeanne smiled. "I've watched Dane. The way he looks at you." She paused and rolled her eyes heavenward. "It makes my engine purr."

"I didn't say he wasn't . . . attracted to me," Annie said awkwardly.

"You'd be lying through your teeth if you did!"

Annie blushed.

"So you think he's just . . . wild about your body?" Jeanne's tone grew softer. "You might not think he cares for you, but I'm sure he does. You should have seen him in the waiting room while you were in surgery. He was sick with worry."

"Perhaps, but I'm sure losing the baby and learning that I couldn't give him more was what he was thinking of."

"What makes you think Dane doesn't love you?" Jeanne took Annie's hand. "Some men aren't good with words, but it doesn't mean they don't care."

Annie regarded her silently for a moment. In a few succinct sentences, she told Jeanne the story of Dane's first marriage. Then she said, "When he proposed to me, he as good as told me that he didn't want to love me, and that he wanted a relationship that didn't include love."

"So you've never told him you love him, either?"

Annie shook her head. "I can't burden him with that, not after...after what happened. He hasn't touched me since the first day in the hospital. I'm sure he wants out of this marriage so he can find a whole woman who can give him children, but he's simply too noble to tell me."

And it was true. He hadn't kissed her, hadn't held her, hadn't touched her in any way except for the most impersonal touches when he had no choice. Like the hand he'd extended to help her into the car from the wheelchair this morning. To her, craving his touch as she did, the mere clasp of his hand had been the most welcome sensation in the world and she'd found it difficult to hide her reaction. He hadn't appeared even to notice.

For once, Jeanne didn't have a ready answer. Her pretty face was troubled as they cleaned up the remains of the lunch she'd brought and after a few more words, she went home while Annie dragged herself upstairs for a nap.

The next six weeks were more of the same. Dane treated her like a convalescent guest in a nursing home. He was unfailingly polite and concerned for her welfare, but he never touched her willingly. He couldn't have made it clearer that he wanted out of the marriage.

They never discussed the baby they'd made together and lost.

It was like the worst sort of torture ever devised, to have to live with him, loving him as she did, and know that someday soon he'd leave.

As her strength returned, she began to walk the dogs again and to visit her canine center, to make plans to return to work full-time. It wasn't what she would have chosen. But Dane didn't want her and the rest of her lonely life would be unbearable if she didn't keep busy.

He knew he couldn't stand the pressure much longer. They were like two strangers, politely touching on the surfaces of each other's lives, backing away before any deeper interchange could occur. Living with her, seeing her pain every day and knowing that she didn't want his comfort was more than he could take.

One evening, he came home from work to see her sitting in the kitchen, staring sightlessly at nothing. When he walked into the room, she made an effort, getting to her feet and walking to the refrigerator.

"Hello. I have a roast in for dinner. Would you like a salad with it?"

"Annie."

"What?" She didn't turn to face him.

He shook his head in frustration. It was like talking to a wall. "Is there some way I can help you?"

She took him literally. "No, thank you. All I have to do is chop some lettuce."

"I didn't mean that." He made an impatient motion with his hand. "Ever since you came home from the hospital, you've barely spoken."

She was silent for a minute more. Then she turned to face him and when her gaze met his, he was seared by the sadness she exuded. "I don't have much to say right now."

As she slipped by him and left the room, he stood with his hands curled into fists of impotence. He was afraid to try to approach her further, when his every overture seemed to only heighten her pain.

He'd hoped that her depression would abate as the weeks passed. But with each new day that dawned, Annie seemed more mired in a private world of stoic grief that he couldn't penetrate. Her fortress was so solidly defended that he didn't dare approach her for even the simplest touch. The infrequent times that she asked him for help or that he was able to assist her left him battling a painful desire so fierce that he had to walk away before he grabbed her and dragged her to him for the embrace he could almost feel.

He found himself more jealous now of her dead husband than he'd ever been in the past, merely because the man had known what it was like to be loved by Annie.

He supposed her withdrawal was understandable. She'd lost so much in her life. Losing the baby had been one blow too many. The glow that always had lit her blue eyes with an inner warmth was gone now, a casualty of her miscarriage and one loss more than she could handle. He'd thought he could refocus her life, bind her to him and create a family and a love that would endure for the rest of their lives.

But he'd been wrong. His love hadn't been enough.

In her room, Annie sat on the edge of the bed, her arms protectively curled over her barren womb. Living with Dane, knowing he was longing for children, was the worst kind of torment she'd ever envisioned. It felt as if she'd lost a husband all over again, though he was still living here in the same house with her.

*She was going to have to offer him his freedom.*

Until now, she hadn't been able to entertain the idea of Dane leaving. Until now, she'd lacked the strength to let him go, even though she knew it would be the right thing to do.

He'd never initiate it, she was positive. He'd married her and even though things had gone sour, he wouldn't back out unless she convinced him that she would be fine alone.

Over breakfast on the day of her six-week checkup, he said, "I've arranged to go in late today."

"Oh?" She glanced at him, but her gaze bounced away without meeting his.

"You need someone to drive you to the doctor."

She flushed slightly. "I was planning on driving myself. I'm sure I'm well enough. You don't have to take time off."

"It's no big deal." She clearly didn't want him to accompany her. But for some reason, he wasn't feeling particularly sensitive today. "What time's your appointment?"

"Ten, but you don't—"

"I said I'd drive you." His tone of voice left no room for argument.

But at ten o'clock, Annie gathered the keys to her van from the hook in the kitchen. "Why don't you follow me? I'm sure I'll get the 'A-okay' to drive again and you won't have to take extra time away from work to bring me home."

He studied her for a moment, realizing that she wasn't going to yield. "All right."

The drive to the doctor's office was short, as was the wait. In what seemed like no time, he was standing in the familiar examining room watching the doctor check Annie.

"Everything looks good, Mrs. Hamilton. You've healed nicely. You can resume normal activity now, including driving and walking. And intercourse." The physician closed his chart and crossed his arms over it. "Have you two considered whether you'd like to try again to have a baby?"

Annie stared at the doctor. "But . . . I can't."

He smiled at her. "You may not be able to conceive in the normal fashion, but you still have a healthy ovary, presumably healthy eggs and a perfectly usable uterus. And a track record of conception. If you're interested, I'll refer you to a fertility specialist who can evaluate you as candidates for an in vitro fertilization program."

"We're not interested," Annie said.

"We're interested." Dane spoke at the same moment. Hope leaped within his breast. He'd resigned himself to a life without children, but he realized that if there was a chance that he and Annie could still have a family, he'd jump at it in a heartbeat, if only to take the shades of sorrow from Annie's eyes.

The doctor was silent for a moment. His eyebrows rose. He and Dane both looked at Annie. She was gazing at the floor and her chin quivered as if she was trying to hold back tears.

"Perhaps you two should discuss this before we make any decisions," the doctor said quietly. "I know losing this baby was difficult. And it's created some challenges, but it doesn't mean your chance to become parents is gone. Think about it and call me." He shook Dane's hand and slipped out of the room.

When the door had closed behind him with a soft whoosh, Dane stepped to Annie's side. She didn't look at him until he placed a gentle forefinger beneath her chin, lifting her face for his inspection.

"Could we please go somewhere and talk? It's important to me," he added, afraid she might shut him out again.

Her shoulders seemed to slump a bit and a tear escaped and went slipping down her cheek. Then she nodded. "All right."

They dropped her van off at the house and he called his secretary to say he wouldn't be coming in. Then he helped Annie into the new sedan and came around to the driver's side. She didn't say a word, not even when he left River Forest and got on the Eisenhower Expressway into Chicago. The silence in the car was thick and oppressive through the entire ride.

Driving around the bottom of the Loop, he passed Grant Park and turned north on Lake Shore Drive, putting the vast, gray expanse of Lake Michigan's Chicago Harbor on their right. The lake looked dark and choppy and cold today, in keeping with the sullen skies that threatened rain. It matched the way he felt inside.

The silence inside the car was absolute. He drove on and on, past Lincoln Park and finally swung the car into a parking spot facing a deserted stretch of beachfront. In the summer, there would be people all over the place, but in late November, the bitter breezes off the lake kept all but the most hardy water-lovers away.

He switched off the engine. They'd be warm enough for a while in the car. Slowly, he pivoted in his seat to face her. "We need to talk."

"I know." Her voice was stifled.

He hesitated, choosing his words with care. "Losing the baby was a big disappointment for you—"

"And an even bigger one for you." He could hear the sorrow in her voice and tears glinted in her eyes as she turned toward him. "Oh, Dane, I'm sorry."

"Annie, you don't have anything to be sorry for." Could she possibly believe he blamed her for something that was no more than rotten biological luck?

"But I do," she whispered, and she looked so stricken he didn't speak, waiting for her to explain. "You were very clear from the beginning that you wanted children, that you were marrying me for one reason . . . to bear your babies. And now you're stuck with a wife who may not be able to give them to you. I know how important it is to you to be able to have children."

"Annie—"

"No, wait." Slowly she drew off the wedding ring and the beautiful sapphire engagement ring he'd given her. "Take these. You need to be free to find a woman who can help you fulfill your dreams."

Dane stared at her, feeling his heart being torn in two as she pressed the rings into his hand.

With a muffled sob, she fumbled for the handle of her door and flung herself out of the car. Before he could react, she was walking away from him, out onto the desolate beach. Her head was down and her shoulders heaved.

The evidence of the grief she was carrying smote him like a blow from a hammer. In that moment, he knew he couldn't bind her to him, force her to acknowledge his presence in her life, when it so clearly brought her painful memories. He should let her go. Blindly, he opened his own door and followed her out onto the sand. "Annie!"

The wind whipped around him. She was far enough ahead of him that the gusts of air snatched his words away and she didn't hear him. He sprinted after her, heedless of the sand shifting beneath his feet, filling his shoes.

Grabbing her elbow, he pulled her to a halt. "Annie, wait."

She tried to turn away but he held her in place with relentless pressure, seeing the tracks of her tears staining her face, feeling each one as an arrow in his heart.

"You can start divorce proceedings tomorrow." His words dropped like stones between them.

If it were possible, her eyes dimmed even more. "Is that what you want me to do?" she asked in a lifeless tone.

The moment was frozen between them, her question echoing with implications. His heart shouted, "Hell, no, that's not what I want!" His brain overruled it, however, and he heard himself cautiously throwing the ball back into her court. "I want you to be happy. Whatever it takes to accomplish that is what I want."

She hesitated.

So did he. He sensed that they were balanced on a knife-edge of change, that his next response could shape his life for the rest of his days. Quietly, shedding his pride and risking his heart, he asked, "Do you want a divorce, Annie?"

The wind howled around them, slapping her braid against her shoulder. She raised her gaze to his face, but for once he couldn't read anything in her expressive eyes. "I want you to be happy," she said. "If you're free, you can look for another woman to have your babies." Her voice quavered at the end, but she didn't look away.

"What if I don't want to be free?"

Annie threw him a pain-filled, incredulous look. "Why wouldn't you?"

"I meant what I said in the hospital, you know." He tried to keep his voice as light and casual as possible. "I don't want any other woman. Children aren't as important to me as keeping you in my life."

She smiled a little then, dislodging a tear, which ran down her cheek and dripped onto the collar of her shirt. "Dane, you want children. I can't give them to you. I appreciate your willingness to be noble, but it isn't necessary."

"I know it's not necessary!" Patience had never been one of his virtues and he was getting sick and tired of trying to make his point. "Dammit, Annie, I'm not being noble. I love you. If you love me, too, we can overcome anything, even not having children of our own."

Her eyes were wide and shocked and he couldn't for the life of him tell what she was thinking. It was too late for graceful exits, he decided. He might as well jump in and say it all. More calmly, he said, "Will you put my rings back on your finger and please answer me?"

Deep down in the depths of her eyes, a tiny blue flame sparked. And in that moment, he dared to hope again. Her lips curved up the tiniest bit in the first real smile he'd seen on her face in weeks. "Could you repeat the question?"

He stared at her for a moment, gauging the slow, deliberate words. He held out the rings, taking her hand in his. "Annie Hamilton, I love you. I want to keep you for my wife, with or without kids. Children would be a great bonus, but they could never replace you. Do you love me?''

Her face grew serious. ''Yes,'' she whispered. Then her voice grew stronger and her eyes began to shine. ''Oh, Dane, I thought you only wanted me for... for...''

''For your reproductive organs?'' He couldn't suppress the chuckle that wanted to burst free as he gently slipped her rings back on her finger.

''Something like that.'' She took his face between her hands. ''I love you. All I want is a life with you.'' She laid her head against his chest. ''And children, if we can have them.''

Dane stroked the length of her braid, reveling in the softness of her body, the silky hair beneath his hand, the warmth of her pressed against him. ''The doctor said we haven't run out of options yet. But I don't want to press you into anything you're not willing to do. All I need to make my life complete is you.''

Annie pulled back a fraction and looked up at him. ''Of course I'm willing to try anything we can to have children.'' Her smile wilted a bit around the edges, but she continued to gaze into his eyes. ''I'll always be sorry our first pregnancy didn't work out. But if the doctors think we stand a chance of trying some alternative methods, I'm all for it.''

She shivered as she finished the last words and he hugged her to him. ''Let's get out of this wind.''

As one, they turned and began walking back toward the car. He kept an arm possessively around her, some part of him fearing that if he didn't hold on to her, all they'd just said might disappear.

Annie laughed, pointing at his feet. "You're going to have to go home and change."

He looked down. His shoes and socks were covered with sand and his gray wool trousers had grains of sand clinging to them, as well. He tightened his arm around her. "Maybe I won't go in to the office at all today."

"Is that an invitation I hear in there?" Her face was glowing, her eyes as warm as he'd wanted to see them for weeks.

"It is." He expanded on the idea that was coming to him. "We owe ourselves some courtship time. Time to be romantic." Stopping just short of the car, he turned to face her, slipping his hands inside her coat and under the long sweater that she wore until his fingers registered the hot, silky texture of woman beneath his hands.

She sighed, snuggling closer to him, slipping her own hands around his back and down to palm his buttocks through his pants. He gasped as her hips tilted into his and he felt the immediate leap of passion rising between them. Annie tilted her face in invitation and he accepted, covering her mouth with his own, tasting the sweet heat he'd been denied for weeks. As he delved deeper into her mouth, his hand slid up to shape and mold her breast.

Annie moaned into his mouth and shivered.

Shivered?

Dane pulled his head back and laughed, straightening her sweater and turning her toward the car again. "How romantic—you're freezing to death."

"But all for a good cause." Annie snuggled closer, kissing the side of his neck as high as she could reach. "Let's go home. I bet a big, strong guy like you has some hot ideas on how to warm me."

# Epilogue

Annie shifted the toddler on her hip as she stood on tiptoe to peer out the kitchen window. "Look, Lizzie, Daddy's home. When Daddy comes in, you can show him the card you made for him today."

The dark-haired tot made a futile lunge at the window as Annie caught her. "Dad-dee! I see Dad-dee!"

Annie set her on the floor. "Run into the den and get your card for Daddy, okay, princess?"

"O-tay!" At twenty-one months, Lizzie didn't know the meaning of the word *walk*. She zipped off toward the den, her little legs pumping as fast as they could go. Annie watched her fondly. *Our little miracle,* Dane called her. And that was exactly how they'd felt when she'd been born nine months after Annie had undergone the process of in vitro fertilization. They'd held their breaths nearly every day of her pregnancy, affected more than either of them cared to admit by the loss of the first baby they'd made together.

Lizzie came screeching back into the kitchen then, and five-year-old Stephen barreled in behind her. Today he was pretending to be a fireman and the red plastic hat he'd gotten during Fire Prevention Week in kindergarten was mashed firmly down atop his unruly white-blond curls.

"Where are your glasses, young man?" Annie asked her son.

"In my room. I'll get 'em, Mommy," he answered, making an abrupt pivot and racing off toward the stairs, the sound of a fire siren trailing behind him. Ebony and Missy, who were his constant companions, loped after him.

They'd made the decision to adopt just last year, though they'd been on a waiting list since shortly after they'd lost the first baby, when they'd gone through the initial paperwork in case their chances for having biological children failed. Stephen, legally blind in one eye as the result of an infection he'd had as an infant, had been overlooked by dozens of adoptive parents, but the moment Dane had seen the little boy, he'd been interested. Lizzie had been less than a year old when they'd first begun to consider adopting additional children and though Annie had assumed they'd be looking for another infant, the four-year-old Stephen had captured her heart the day she'd first seen him in the foster home where they'd gone to see two infants.

"Would you take me home?" he'd asked Dane, climbing into his lap without reservation. "I need a daddy and a mommy."

She'd been touched to tears, she recalled, and Dane had been nearly unable to respond to the hopeful child. They'd gone home that night and discussed it.

"The placement officer says the babies are much easier to place, and that she has a waiting list," Annie had said tentatively to Dane. "That dear little Stephen was certainly a character, wasn't he?"

Dane had nodded. "I imagine with his vision problems, he won't be first on anyone's list." Then he'd turned to her and his gaze had been hopeful. "Except maybe ours. How would you feel about adopting a child that's older?"

They'd applied to adopt Stephen the very next day and he'd come home with them a short month later for a trial period. Adjusting to having a very lively little boy in addition to a baby had been . . . interesting, she recalled with a smile, but they'd never been sorry. And she knew that Dane would always feel especially happy to have made a difference in another lonely child's life.

Her only regret was that they hadn't had Stephen from the day he'd been given up. All she had from the first four years of his life were a few pictures that had been taken for adoption portfolios over the years and a tattered teddy bear that he'd only recently felt secure enough to sleep without.

As Lizzie came rushing back into the kitchen with a grubby piece of paper clutched in her fist, Dane opened the back door.

"Dad-dee!" shrieked the little girl, hurling herself at him.

Dane stooped just in time to catch her, setting his briefcase aside and rising with Lizzie in his arms.

"How's my princess today?" he asked her. "Were you Mommy's helper?"

Lizzie nodded solemnly. "Made din-ner. 'Tephen he'p."

Dane pretended amazement. "You and Stephen made dinner? Wow. I can't wait to taste it." He took the paper that Lizzie was shoving at him. "What's this?"

"Card. Mom-mee he'p 'Izzie."

Dane looked at the scribbled crayon marks covering the dog-eared sheet. "I love you, Daddy," he solemnly read aloud. "This is a beautiful card, Lizzie. You did a good job."

He looked over her head at Annie. "Hi, Mommy. Thank you for helping Lizzie with her card."

The little girl squirmed to be set down and he complied, coming over to link his arms around Annie's waist and pull her into his arms. "How's my number one princess?" he asked softly.

She smiled up into his eyes, still as blue as the day they'd met, though he was getting a few silver strands in the dark hair near his temples. "Just fine," she said.

"Busy day?"

She smiled wryly. "If changing diapers, building with blocks, carpooling three kindergarteners to school and back, picking up the party invitations from the printers and teaching two Basic classes while Stephen was in school and Lizzie was at the baby-sitter's counts, yes, you could say I was busy.''

"How do the invitations look?"

"Very nice." She leaned into him. "If you'll help me address them this weekend, we'll be in pretty good shape. I already have a tentative menu planned for our annual spring cocktail party."

Dane pressed a leisurely kiss onto her mouth, lingering to taste the sweetness inside. "What a hostess. All that work, and you even have dinner ready. Is that why I love you?"

"No." She leaned into him and deliberately brushed her hips back and forth against him, over and over again. "Maybe later I'll remind you."

A clatter of little feet accompanied by the tick-tack of dog toenails on the tiled floor warned them that Stephen and the dogs were about to descend for their own greetings. "I'm going to count on that reminder," he said in a husky voice, "even though that's only one of the reasons I love you."

And he released her to greet his son.

\* \* \* \* \*

## FREE TV 3268 DRAW RULES
## NO PURCHASE OR OBLIGATION NECESSARY

# JINGLE BELLS, WEDDING BELLS:
## Silhouette's Christmas Collection for 1994

---

### Christmas Wish List

*To beat the crowds at the malls and get the perfect present for *everyone,* even that snoopy Mrs. Smith next door!

*To get through the holiday parties without running my panty hose.

*To bake cookies, decorate the house and serve the perfect Christmas dinner—just like the women in all those magazines.

*To sit down, curl up and read my Silhouette Christmas stories!

---

Join *New York Times* bestselling author Nora Roberts, along with popular writers Barbara Boswell, Myrna Temte and Elizabeth August, as we celebrate the joys of Christmas—and the magic of marriage—with

## JINGLE BELLS, WEDDING BELLS

### Silhouette's Christmas Collection for 1994.

JBWB

## Jilted!
### They were left at the altar...
### but not for long!

**#889  THE ACCIDENTAL BRIDEGROOM—Ann Major**
November's *Man of the Month* Rafe Steele never thought one night with Cathy Calderon would make him a father. Now he had to find her before she married someone else!

**#890  TWO HEARTS, SLIGHTLY USED—Dixie Browning**
*Outer Banks*
Frances Jones discovered the way to win sexy Brace Ridgeway was through his stomach—until he got the flu and couldn't eat! But by then, Brace only craved a sweet dessert called Frances....

**#891  THE BRIDE SAYS NO—Cait London**
Clementine Barlow gave rancher Evan Tanner a "Dear John" letter from her sister, breaking their engagement. Even though the bride said no, will this sister say yes?

**#892  SORRY, THE BRIDE HAS ESCAPED—Raye Morgan**
Ashley Carrington couldn't marry without love, so she ran off on her wedding day. Was Kam Caine willing to risk falling in love to give this former bride a chance?

**#893  A GROOM FOR RED RIDING HOOD—Jennifer Greene**
After being left at the altar, Mary Ellen Barnett knew she couldn't trust anyone. Especially the wolf that lay underneath Steve Rawlings's sexy exterior....

**#894  BRIDAL BLUES—Cathie Linz**
When Nick Grant came back home, Melissa Carlson enlisted his help to win back her ex-fiancé. But once she succeeded, she realized it was Nick she wanted to cure her bridal blues!

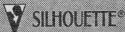

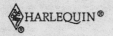 HARLEQUIN®

## The movie event of the season can be the reading event of the year!

Lights… The lights go on in October when CBS presents Harlequin/Silhouette Sunday Matinee Movies. These four movies are based on bestselling Harlequin and Silhouette novels.

Camera… As the cameras roll, be the first to read the original novels the movies are based on!

Action… Through this offer, you can have these books sent directly to you! Just fill in the order form below and you could be reading the books…before the movie!

| | | | |
|---|---|---|---|
| 48288-4 | Treacherous Beauties by Cheryl Emerson | $3.99 U.S./$4.50 CAN. | ☐ |
| 83305-9 | Fantasy Man by Sharon Green | $3.99 U.S./$4.50 CAN. | ☐ |
| 48289-2 | A Change of Place by Tracy Sinclair | $3.99 U.S./$4.50CAN. | ☐ |
| 83306-7 | Another Woman by Margot Dalton | $3.99 U.S./$4.50 CAN. | ☐ |

|   |   |
|---|---|
| **TOTAL AMOUNT** | $ |
| **POSTAGE & HANDLING** | $ |
| ($1.00 for one book, 50¢ for each additional) | |
| **APPLICABLE TAXES*** | $ _____ |
| **TOTAL PAYABLE** | $ _____ |
| (check or money order—please do not send cash) | |

To order, complete this form and send it, along with a check or money order for the total above, payable to Harlequin Books, to: **In the U.S.:** 3010 Walden Avenue, P.O. Box 9047, Buffalo, NY 14269-9047; **In Canada:** P.O. Box 613, Fort Erie, Ontario, L2A 5X3.

Name: _____

Address: _____ City: _____

State/Prov.: _____ Zip/Postal Code: _____

*New York residents remit applicable sales taxes.
 Canadian residents remit applicable GST and provincial taxes.                    CBSPR

# "HOORAY FOR HOLLYWOOD" SWEEPSTAKES

## HERE'S HOW THE SWEEPSTAKES WORKS

### OFFICIAL RULES — NO PURCHASE NECESSARY

To enter, complete an Official Entry Form or hand print on a 3" x 5" card the words "HOORAY FOR HOLLYWOOD", your name and address and mail your entry in the pre-addressed envelope (if provided) or to: "Hooray for Hollywood" Sweepstakes, P.O. Box 9076, Buffalo, NY 14269-9076 or "Hooray for Hollywood" Sweepstakes, P.O. Box 637, Fort Erie, Ontario L2A 5X3. Entries must be sent via First Class Mail and be received no later than 12/31/94. No liability is assumed for lost, late or misdirected mail.

Winners will be selected in random drawings to be conducted no later than January 31, 1995 from all eligible entries received.

Grand Prize: A 7-day/6-night trip for 2 to Los Angeles, CA including round trip air transportation from commercial airport nearest winner's residence, accommodations at the Regent Beverly Wilshire Hotel, free rental car, and $1,000 spending money. (Approximate prize value which will vary dependent upon winner's residence: $5,400.00 U.S.); 500 Second Prizes: A pair of "Hollywood Star" sunglasses (prize value: $9.95 U.S. each). Winner selection is under the supervision of D.L. Blair, Inc., an independent judging organization, whose decisions are final. Grand Prize travelers must sign and return a release of liability prior to traveling. Trip must be taken by 2/1/96 and is subject to airline schedules and accommodations availability.

Sweepstakes offer is open to residents of the U.S. (except Puerto Rico) and Canada who are 18 years of age or older, except employees and immediate family members of Harlequin Enterprises, Ltd., its affiliates, subsidiaries, and all agencies, entities or persons connected with the use, marketing or conduct of this sweepstakes. All federal, state, provincial, municipal and local laws apply. Offer void wherever prohibited by law. Taxes and/or duties are the sole responsibility of the winners. Any litigation within the province of Quebec respecting the conduct and awarding of prizes may be submitted to the Regie des loteries et courses du Quebec. All prizes will be awarded; winners will be notified by mail. No substitution of prizes are permitted. Odds of winning are dependent upon the number of eligible entries received.

Potential grand prize winner must sign and return an Affidavit of Eligibility within 30 days of notification. In the event of non-compliance within this time period, prize may be awarded to an alternate winner. Prize notification returned as undeliverable may result in the awarding of prize to an alternate winner. By acceptance of their prize, winners consent to use of their names, photographs, or likenesses for purpose of advertising, trade and promotion on behalf of Harlequin Enterprises, Ltd., without further compensation unless prohibited by law. A Canadian winner must correctly answer an arithmetical skill-testing question in order to be awarded the prize.

For a list of winners (available after 2/28/95), send a separate stamped, self-addressed envelope to: Hooray for Hollywood Sweepstakes 3252 Winners, P.O. Box 4200, Blair, NE 68009.

CBSRLS

## OFFICIAL ENTRY COUPON

# "Hooray for Hollywood"
## SWEEPSTAKES!

Yes, I'd love to win the Grand Prize — a vacation in Hollywood — or one of 500 pairs of "sunglasses of the stars"! Please enter me in the sweepstakes!

This entry must be received by December 31, 1994.
Winners will be notified by January 31, 1995.

Name _____

Address _____ Apt. _____

City _____

State/Prov. _____ Zip/Postal Code _____

Daytime phone number _____
(area code)

Mail all entries to: Hooray for Hollywood Sweepstakes,
P.O. Box 9076, Buffalo, NY 14269-9076.
In Canada, mail to: Hooray for Hollywood Sweepstakes,
P.O. Box 637, Fort Erie, ON L2A 5X3.

KCH